The Curse

The Curse

Jennifer Brassel

Published by Jennifer Brassel, 2019.

The Curse
Jennifer Brassel

Seth Almose has spent many lives trying to break a curse that robs his family of their soul mates. Meeting Julia Morrow signals the cycle has begun again.

After fleeing a stalker who has made her wary of men, Julia refuses to believe Seth's stories of reincarnation and family curses. But her dreams are telling her otherwise.

How can Seth convince Julia to put aside her misgivings and admit she is his reborn lover, before it is too late?

About the author

Jennifer Brassel is passionate about a lot of things: romance, history and mythology to name but a few, and writing allows her imagination to run riot. Creative to the bone, when Jennifer isn't writing she can be seen with a paintbrush in hand. She also has a special love for the history of ancient Egypt and had she not beome an author, she'd likely have ended up at archaeological digs instead.

Historical fiction is her first love and her work has won a number of major romance writing contests including: Land of Enchantment Romance Writers (*Rebecca*), From The Heart Romance Writers (*Wallflower*) and Missouri Romance Writers of America (*Gateway to the Best*).

Jennifer holds an MA in Creative Writing and teaches writing courses and workshops for community colleges and writing centres, as well as doing historical research at one of Australia's premier universities.

Married to her high school sweetheart, most of her days are spent staring at her computer screen under the supervision of a very demanding bichon frisé, Cordy.

First published by Harlequin Australia in 2014
Copyright © 2014 Jennifer Brassel
Revised edition 2019
All rights reserved

JENNIFER BRASSEL

For Lellie

"A curse upon your house and all your descendants. May you never keep those you hold dear safe. May you ever lose them and die of loneliness. I pledge on my ka, and by your gods and mine, my descendants will return to thwart yours through all eternity until you surrender your entire kingdom ..."

Enlil of Sechem,
C1480 BCE

Special note to readers:

This work is the companion book to *Warrior King*, published by Trifecta Publishing House, and while it isn't necessary, it is helpful to read *Warrior King* prior to this book. The characters of *Warrior King*, Alia and Menkhepere, are close to my heart, and inspired this book that explores reincarnation and love across the boundaries of time.

Warrior King is available, in digital and print, through all good book retailers.

Jennifer Brassel

Prologue

San Francisco,

    A year ago

"You can't mean it!" Celine cried, her dark eyes flashing up at him. "You don't know what you're saying. All that reincarnation stuff. It's rubbish! Rubbish, I tell you."

"Uncle Salman was adamant–"

"You're a grown man," she cut in. "You know there's no such thing as a soul mate – it's all tripe – the kind of rubbish sprouted by those new age types so they can sell their dinky books. Your uncle was just telling bedtime stories. You can't honestly say you believed all that guff about ancient prophesies and curses."

Seth sighed and rubbed his temple. This wasn't going well. But he owed her an explanation.

"Whether you think it's rubbish or not, it doesn't matter. Just believe me when I say I know you're not the one. I thought you might have been, but now I'm sure. I'm sorry, Celine." He took her hand and tried to soothe her anger with one of his warm smiles, but she wrenched away and turned from him to stare out over the moonlit expanse of black water.

"You could love me if you wanted to."

Again Seth sighed. His eyes drifted over the beautiful woman before him as he tried to find the right words to make her understand. But there were none. It was patently clear she didn't want to understand.

"If you believe that – then you don't really know what love is."

She turned and smiled that intimate little smile she reserved only for him, and whispered sweetly, "How would you know, darling? You said yourself that you've never been in love. You can't be sure, one way or another, until you've truly tasted what my love might have to offer.

We've only slept together once and that was weeks ago. A grown man cannot remain a virtual celibate indefinitely – it's not healthy."

Stepping closer, she slid her hands up his lapels and circled his shoulders, pressing herself against him – a sinuous and unmistakable invitation. The look on her face became almost predatory as she moved to place soft, open-mouthed kisses along his neck, just below his ear. "What you're looking for doesn't exist," she murmured as her eyes closed and her hand began to slide downward. "Love *grows* – you could learn to love me."

It was his turn to pull away. "Don't," he said as he gently removed her arms and took a pace backward. "It won't work – it wasn't meant to be."

Her eyes narrowed until they were dark slits and all her beauty seemed to melt into nothing.

He glanced away. This wasn't how he'd envisaged it ending between them. It wasn't her fault, but at the same time he couldn't help how he felt. And to take their relationship any further would only make the lie bigger. Ending it harder.

Still, he had to try.

"I wish I could say it might happen, but I know it won't. I have to find her. If it takes my entire life, I have to find her."

"Go then. Damned well go and search half the country! See if you can find your precious soul mate, but," she gave him a savage stare, "I bet you won't.

"It's a stupid pipe-dream, a fairytale – and you're a fool if you think otherwise. No man in his right mind can deny his needs for the sake of some stupid curse."

For long seconds their eyes clashed in silent confrontation before she turned away and marched across the spacious living room to fling the front door open with a violent sweep of her arm.

"Go!" she screeched, "– and when you get tired of your ridiculous quest, don't expect me to be here waiting because I won't be. I don't need you, Seth Almose. Get, the hell, out. *Go!*"

"I'm sorry," he repeated as he grabbed his car keys and cell-phone from the table, "I didn't want it to be like this. I'd hoped you would understand."

With her lips pressed to a thin, angry line, she turned her face away as if the sight of him disgusted her.

Knowing there was nothing more to say, he went.

The door shook as it slammed behind him . . .

*

Jamaica Plain, Boston
Six months ago ...
With his coat collar tugged high about his neck, the watcher hunched on the bench at the bus stop across the street from Julia Morrow's second floor apartment. It was one of his favorite places, he could see her moving about her small studio but the throngs of tourist traffic and a nearby tree shielded him from nosey onlookers. He always wore dark clothes and sunglasses, just to be certain none of the neighbors noticed him.

Over the past year he'd spent many weeks on this bench. Months even. He liked to sit and keep watch – it made him feel closer to her, more connected. He'd lost count of the number of times he'd waved the bus on as it slowed to pick him up.

As he studied the play of shadows on the blind covered window, he considered his options. He knew he'd have to make a move soon. But it was difficult to find an excuse to approach her. Several times he'd come close, but circumstances held him back. Or someone interfered.

He remembered the moment he first saw her – in that instant he knew she belonged to him; they were destined to be together. But her reaction when she'd fled Australia had made him more cautious. This time she wouldn't recognize him until he was ready for her, until all his plans were in place. So he sat vigil and waited until the time ripened.

Ah – there! She stood by the window now; he could see her clearly outlined by the glow of the lights. His body stirred, and he smiled to himself as he shifted on the hard wooden bench to ease the pressure at his groin. Tightening the belt of his coat, he sat up straighter and tried to get a better look. Yes. It'd have to be soon. Her escape had cost him much time already. He didn't think he'd be able to hold out much longer.

Maybe his new friends would provide the means?

*

Inscription, Tomb 100, Rekh-mi-re, Vizier, Tuthmosis III, Sheikh Abd el-Qurna, Theban Necropolis:

Behold! I am he who my King commanded to supervise the red land and black land.

Behold! I brought back the hostages after the defeat of the Retennu peoples,

the princes and princesses who will ensure allegiance of the subjugated lands...

One

Four weeks ago ....

He was staring straight at her – Julia could feel it.

Her gaze darted across the room until it came to rest on the photograph. A shiver arced up her spine as the ancient face called to her as loudly as if he'd cried out her name.

With a frustrated scrub of her face, she stood and flexed her stiff knees.

Ever since she'd been to the exhibit, the photograph had beckoned and taunted. Even now her eyes were drawn to the black and white image pinned to the cork message board by the door. Deep in the back of Julia's mind there existed a preternatural knowing; the statue meant something – something significant about the man personified in the stone. Something she knew she ought to remember, but it danced at the very edge of her memory and she couldn't bring it into focus.

Every time she looked up, the face seemed to plead 'paint me, paint me....' and as she glanced down at the paintbrush in her hand, she knew she'd have to do just that. Never mind the landscape Irene commissioned months ago for a showing that loomed only days away. This was more compelling. More inspiring.

And perhaps, once she'd finished, she could sleep again because since she'd developed that photograph, she hadn't been able to really rest. Even in her dreams, what little she recalled, he whispered to her of things she didn't want to remember.

She picked up her palette and went to stand before the large white canvas sitting atop her easel. "So you want me to paint your portrait, do you?" she said to the photograph as if it had openly challenged her. "All right then, my friend – let's see how you come up in glorious living color."

With that, she began to block in the basic shapes and tones she saw in the photograph. Julia didn't notice the time passing as she worked.

This was always a crucial phase – when she sought, and usually found, the living essence that lay beneath the two-dimensional rendering. Her hand moved with precision, almost of its own volition.

And her pharaoh didn't disappoint her.

The face came to life within a few short hours and when she finally put her brush aside, she was astounded by what she'd done. He was beautiful. Simply beautiful. So much more than the photograph. And Julia had an eerie gut feeling that she'd come very close to capturing the spirit of the man who'd lived all those thousands of years ago.

Stepping back, she allowed herself to study the canvas with a critical eye. Though still raw, there was no denying it – it held a potential, a feeling she hadn't experienced in her own work for quite a while.

"I wonder," she mused, "did you guide me?" She directed her question to the photograph, which of course remained mute, but she couldn't help smiling all the same. Whether by accident or design, she knew this painting would be one of her best. Emotions were bound up within the image, and those emotions literally leapt from his eyes.

Threading her fingers through her wheat-colored hair, she glanced at the advertising poster that hung alongside the photograph. Today was the last day the exhibit would be open to the public. Her final chance to look upon that beguiling face.

Did she dare go back? She knew she didn't really have time – there were three wedding shoots to print up. She'd made quite a name for herself locally by concentrating on old-fashioned black and white photography using film. Of course she also used digital, especially for color work, but she'd found there was still a good market for the black and white.

But the face pinned to the wall called to her and she couldn't ignore his summons.

As she stepped out onto the sidewalk, the bus that would take her to the Museum of Fine Arts pulled up at the curb. Her breath caught as she noticed the giant poster on its side, the very same poster that had brought her here this morning.

"It's just a coincidence," she murmured to herself in the hope that none of what she'd experienced over the past few days was in any way paranormal. She didn't believe in that stuff. At least, she didn't want to. But she was certain that if she told Irene the whole story, her *avant garde* agent would have some mighty strange explanations to offer.

An inexplicable excitement bubbled in her chest as she paid for her ticket then headed straight for the floor where the exhibit was located. Something deep inside urged her to hurry and when she entered the exhibition rooms, she sighed when found herself almost alone with the relics of an age long gone. Like an automaton, she moved in the direction of the room devoted to Tuthmosis III, and once inside, she relaxed as the sense of urgency left her. For some reason, one she didn't begin to understand, she felt at home within this place, amongst these artifacts.

At the very centre of the room stood the life-sized statue of the dead king, encased in glass and lit from above. She spent quite some time studying the other items in their display cases in a deliberate attempt to stop herself feeling so drawn to the statue. But as she slowly edged closer her whole body began to tingle with anticipation – she needed to go to him – like a siren, he called to her.

Running her fingers across the glass, she wished she could reach out to touch the cold stone and feel the life trapped within the image. Her mind flew back to her painting; if the statue was any indication, she'd faithfully caught his soul on canvas. Both were the embodiment of him. How she knew this was beyond all reckoning, yet, instinctively, she knew it to be true. A sense of rightness, an inner warmth, flooded her. The minutes ticked by as her eyes clung to the carved face, drawn, as if by magic.

"He be wonderful," came a thickly accented voice from behind her.

Startled, Julia's head turned sharply. A short, rotund man in a gray uniform grinned at her. She could see in an instant that he was one of the Egyptian security guards who accompanied the exhibit.

"I wasn't trying to damage anything," she offered as she drew her hand sheepishly away. Her palm print remained on the glass as a clear indictment.

He chuckled. "Don't alarm you self, miss. A cleaning peoples, a lady, she comes to polish lots of times all days. Many peoples do this on glass case. Is tribute to Great One that peoples wants to be close and touch."

"Yes, I suppose it is," Julia observed as she turned back to the statue and once again became transfixed. "It was all so long ago ... and yet ... he seems almost alive."

"Is way for some peoples. In my country, they says the dynasty never die. Some peoples believe his family lives still, even now."

"Do you think so?" Julia asked, though she didn't take her eyes from the statue's enigmatic face.

"Some peoples think it. Me? I no sure." He glanced across the room to a dark corner where another man, a tall man, stood wrapped in shadow. "But some peoples think it," he repeated.

Julia's eyes shot to the security guard, sensing his words held a greater meaning, but his grinning face appeared guileless and honest.

"I guess I can't stand here staring at this statue all day." *No matter how much I want to.* "Pardon me," she said as she made to step by, yet unable to stop her gaze returning to the ancient face. She knew her reaction bordered on the ridiculous – after all, it was only a lump of carved stone – yet somehow she couldn't help herself.

With the guard trailing behind, she started for the exit but as she reached it she couldn't resist turning back one last time, to take a final look. Her footsteps slowed. Intellectually she knew she should leave, but it seemed so hard, knowing she was unlikely to ever set eyes upon the statue again.

She let her eyelids drift closed as she held her breath, willing the statue's hold to loosen until she felt strong enough to walk away.

"Do you know where I can buy a catalogue?" she asked the guard as she forced herself to cross the threshold – a strange sense of loss weighing heavily.

"Yes, miss, in the cafe," he pointed to a lighted niche beyond the exhibit, "there, downs end corridor. Free Turkish coffee if you buys book. And baklava, she is good. You try." He kissed his fingertips in a gesture of sheer gastronomic delight.

"Thanks, I might just do that," she replied, feigning enthusiasm. She detested the taste of honey so baklava would be the last thing she'd sample. She only kept it in her cupboard for guests, or Bird. Still, coffee sounded just what she needed.

Moments later, mocha in hand, Julia sat at a table and flipped through the pages of the catalogue. She'd neglected to buy it the first time around because she'd honestly thought she wasn't interested. She'd only tagged along as company for Irene.

How Irene'd laugh if she knew that Julia had visited the exhibit twice since then.

A number of glossy pages were devoted to her pharaoh and several amulets and a necklace from his treasure stole her attention. She smoothed her fingers across the photograph as if she were touching the blue stones of the necklace. It was almost as if she had run her fingertips across them before.

And the ring. A small silver bird-of-prey. She could almost feel it encircling her left thumb and the urge to rub the empty spot was so strong, her hand felt naked without it.

The fine hairs at the back of her neck began to prickle. She scanned the busy café as she flipped the page. She didn't see the man – the same man who'd kept to the shadows in the exhibit – now sat at a table behind her.

So engrossed in the images before her Julia saw nothing beyond it, and her coffee had cooled by the time she blindly took a sip. She drank the strong brew straight down, but it was too late to give her the pick-me-up she sought and she didn't even try to stifle an unladylike yawn.

The frenzied night of painting had suddenly caught up.

I'd better go home and get some sleep if I'm to have any hope of finishing those two wedding collages by the deadline.

As she walked away she cast a glance back towards the exhibition rooms. An inexplicable sense of sadness filled her chest – as if she were being forced to say goodbye to someone she'd known intimately ... someone attached to her heart ... and the feeling of grief was as real and compelling as if that statue was a living, breathing ... dare she think it – lover?

*

The man, who wore dark, reflective sunglasses, stood shortly after the woman left the café and followed at a discreet distance. *There was something about her ...*

At the entrance to the museum, he paused and studied her progress as she stepped onto the route 39. He hailed himself a cab.

"Just follow the bus for the moment," he told the driver. At each stop, the man leaned out the window to watch for her, and when she finally climbed off the bus on Centre Street, he ordered the cab to pull over.

"I'll return in a minute or two – please stay here," he commanded.

"It's your money, pal," the driver replied.

On the sidewalk, he sauntered along at an easy pace and allowed the woman to move further ahead, but he never quite lost sight of her. When she turned into an apartment building, he wandered past as if taking an afternoon stroll.

Only a small block, perhaps six apartments, he guessed, from the number of mailboxes nestled in the narrow entry between a bookstore and art supply. No names, though.

With a nod of satisfaction, he returned to the cab and drove off.

*

Opening the letter Seth muttered a string of profanities under his breath and reached for his cell. Rick answered on the second ring.

"Yes, Boss."

"In my office," Seth growled without preamble. "I just received another one."

Careful to touch only the very corner of the paper he read and reread the latest cut-and-paste warning letter as he waited for his personal security expert. Although their offices were on separate floors the man arrived within less than two minutes.

Rick didn't wait for an explanation. "What does this one say?" he asked, snatching the letter from Seth's hand and lifting his glasses so he could examine the letter closely.

"What about fingerprints?" Seth asked with a deep frown. "Shouldn't you be wearing gloves?"

"Our blackmailer hasn't left any on the other notes. Why do you think he will change his M.O. now? Don't worry, I'll get it tested but I doubt it'll do any good. Same paper, same threats ...," he peered at the pasted squares, "and looks like he's using the same magazine for his cut-outs."

Your fault. You will pay. You will lose like I have lost.

Seth drew in a deep breath and let it out very slowly. "Have you had any luck with the investor file? Or found any former client who could have lost everything and wants to blame the bank? Maybe a disgruntled employee?"

Easing into the chair across the giant desk, Rick shook his head. "I've checked and double-checked and can't find anyone who fits the bill. Edward has also gone over all the audit statements. There's nothing."

Nothing. Seth was beginning to get a headache from all this. The man, whoever he was, had sent four letters in all. No demands. No specific threats. No hints as to the reason for the letters. Just the vague threat that he *would lose like I have lost*. If it wasn't for the fact that each letter was marked 'Private and confidential' and addressed to Seth personally, they would have assumed it was just someone's idea of a sick joke. But an inner sense of foreboding made Seth just a little edgy. Considering the curse on his family, he couldn't help but feel wary.

"Get the thing to the police, Rick. It's all we can do until he does something concrete."

"That's what worries me – nutcases like this, when they make their move, are often deadly. I'd like to keep a security detail on you—"

Seth raised his hand and shook his head vehemently, his thick, ebony ponytail fanning out across his shoulder. "You know how I feel about that, Rick."

"But we need to take precautions."

"Maybe so, but I am not going to be cosseted by a bunch of karate mad guards. It's ridiculous," his golden gaze snapping at Rick, he leaned over the desk, "and don't think I haven't noticed the man you have following me. He is about as subtle as a bear at a picnic."

Rick just shrugged and waved the latest note under his Seth's nose. "I'll get this to the police crime lab and see if they can find anything useful. Meanwhile you should watch your back. The notes are coming quicker now, which might mean he'll escalate soon. And it wouldn't hurt to increase the security here at the bank for a while, just in case."

Seth leaned back in his chair and sighed. "Do what you think we need to – except the personal detail," his eyes held a distinct warning as Rick stood to leave.

"But–"

"Forget it – I'm feeling claustrophobic as it is. I'll just have to take my chances."

"Whatever you say."

*

Julia woke with a start. Sweat lathered her forehead and her sheets were tangled about her legs. She'd been dreaming again. The dream itself had already faded to just a shadow, but she knew it was another like those she'd experienced in recent days. All she remembered was the eyes – golden eyes – filled with sadness and clouded by darkness.

Sitting up, she peered at the digital readout of her alarm clock, rubbing her face as she tried to focus on the blurred green numbers. Only 4.48 a.m. Dawn was still a long way off, and though she didn't quite remember her dream, something threatening in it had brought her startlingly awake.

What? She had no idea.

After a trip to the bathroom, Julia pulled on her light house-coat and padded to the kitchen. The Egyptian's eyes followed her every step of the way and it took a supreme effort of will on her part not to look at the photograph. Her mind strayed to the covered canvas on its easel across the other side of the room. She'd worked furiously, late into the night, and made great progress. Perhaps, after she'd drunk her tea she'd paint a little more before heading back to bed.

Cup in hand, she flipped on the small lamp, sat cross-legged on the sofa and sighed. Why she wanted to avoid seeing the photograph, she didn't really know, but the more she felt compelled to look, the more she wanted to fight that compulsion.

"Who *are* you?" she asked in quiet frustration once she realized she'd already lost the battle and glanced up at the corkboard. Without words, without intent, this long-dead pharaoh had cast a spell upon her and seemed to constantly whisper to her in ways she couldn't explain. The urge to paint him became overwhelming. Maybe she'd discuss it with Irene when she came for dinner and collect the last of the photographs for the show. But what could she say that'd make any sense? Irene'd probably just laugh hysterically and advise she needed a lover — Irene's answer for everything.

With another sigh, she turned on the halogen spotlights she'd positioned above her easel so she could work at night. Then she dragged a dining chair across the room, and, standing on its wooden seat, pointed a down light directly at the photograph.

The sun had risen quite high by the time she put down her brush and focused on the painting as a whole. She'd finished! In her frenzy she'd gotten paint all over her clothes, her hands were covered too, but she'd finished – and it felt as if some great burden had lifted. Slumping back into a chair, she stared from the photograph to the painting and back again. He took her breath away. Literally. How she'd managed it she didn't begin to understand, but the face that looked back from the canvas had sprung to life. She'd almost swear a living, breathing person had posed and she'd somehow captured the very essence of his personality.

A vague sensation passed through her – a release. Had she been possessed for the time it took to execute the painting?

*

"Stuffaduck … stuffaduck! Give us a kiss, sweetheart!"

"Hey, Bird," Julia answered as she pushed the front door closed. "I really wish Grant hadn't taught you that." She placed the carry bag containing her fresh bread and milk on the table and approached the perch where her Australian, *Major Mitchell* parrot sat dancing to music no one else could hear. Bending down, she let the large pink bird preen her cheek and ear. "Of all the ridiculous things for my dopey brother to teach you, it had to be something embarrassing. What's wrong with 'Polly want a cracker'?" she asked the bird, who simply went about its preening and tried to grab clumps of hair to chew on.

"Uh—uh," she pulled the long, pale strands out of harm's way. "It's bad enough you have to curse and carry on, but you're not going to make me bald as well," she chided playfully.

The parrot rested its face against her cheek as if hugging her while she stroked his pink and white tail. "Yeah, I love you too, Bird."

"Stuffaduck!"

She stood and furrowed her brow. Perhaps if she gave him a name other than 'Bird', he might start saying that instead. It was certainly worth a try.

Fetching seed and fresh water, she fed the parrot and allowed it to sit on her shoulder while she changed the paper at the base of the perch. "No pulling hair, you," she admonished as the bird settled beside her ear. "If you behave, I might even find a nice lettuce leaf for you to munch on."

After drizzling a little honey on a leaf of lettuce, she returned Bird to his perch and rested the leaf on a tray beside the stand. "There you go. While you eat that, I'm going to have a bit of a nap. So no mess, please."

In her bedroom, she pulled down the blind, stripped off her jeans and threw on a big t-shirt before diving onto the mattress and curling into a ball. Although it was warm and sunny outside, her room remained quite cool all year round as the sun rarely touched its window. "Mm—mmm—mmm," she crooned as she felt her mind slipping from consciousness. She had nowhere to be and no one to answer to. She could sleep the rest of the day away if she wanted.

The dream returned as if she had never left it.

*

"Two pizzas?" Julia commented as she swung the door wide. "Who else did you invite?"

Irene waltzed past in her bright red pantsuit, flourishing two flat boxes and a bottle of wine. "I thought I'd take pity on you and get one without anchovies; it wouldn't be prudent to upset my premier artist only days before her first major showing."

With a broad smile Julia closed the door. "I guess you know which side your bread is buttered. What have you got for me? Not something else as disgusting as salty little fish, I hope."

"You wish," Irene winked, then turned and noticed the painting. *"Ohmygod!"*

Only quick thinking on Julia's part saved their dinner from landing in a sludgy pile on the floor.

A choked sound escaped Irene's throat as she rushed over to take a closer look. "Oh, Julia, this is truly amazing – the best you've ever done! He seems so real and life-like—" she peered closer to study the face in detail, "—I could almost touch him." She turned to look at Julia, clearly astonished. "It's so intimate. I don't recognize him – who posed – anyone I know?"

Julia nodded at the photograph on the wall. "It's him."

Eyes wide, Irene didn't hide her disbelief. "But you must have had a model ... it's too natural. He's too real."

Crossing her arms, Julia shook her head. "Nope. The only inspiration was the photograph. I don't know what it was precisely, but it spoke to me ... like he begged me to paint him. And once I started," she shrugged, embarrassed that her explanation sounded so inadequate, "I couldn't stop until it was done. I've barely slept for two days, and when I did ... "

She let the sentence hang. She didn't quite know what happened in those dreams, but she suspected they were significant – that this whole experience had significance. She knew she was meant to go to the museum yesterday, just as she was meant to go that first time with Irene when she took the photo. And therein lay another puzzle. The attendant had seen her take it ... of that, she was certain. But he hadn't stopped her, hadn't tried to confiscate her film, even though there were signs everywhere prohibiting the use of cameras. Weird.

"Well," Irene said, breaking into Julia's thoughts. "This is going to fetch a pretty penny at the showing."

Julia's mouth dropped open. "But you can't put it into the show. It isn't framed and the catalogue is already being printed."

With a calculating expression, Irene waved away Julia's argument. "So? I can advertise it as a surprise – that'll get the critics' tongues wagging."

Taking a deep breath, Julia grabbed a cotton throw-over and covered the painting. She hadn't contemplated beyond finishing the portrait and she certainly hadn't expected Irene would suggest including it in the show. "I'm not sure I want to sell it."

"What? You're kidding me, right?"

Julia grimaced.

"But you can't let me see something like this and then say it's not for sale." Raising herself to her full height, she rounded on Julia, her blue eyes blazing. "Are you insane?"

Backing up a step, Julia turned away. "I didn't say it *wasn't* for sale – I'm just not sure. I can't really explain it, Irene. All I know is, this painting means more to me than anything I've done before and it ... " She looked across at Irene wishing she could make some sense of the jumbled feelings running through her. "I just don't know ..."

Irene's bright red lips curved into a broad smile. "How about we make a deal? I'll include the painting and open it to offers, but it's up to you to decide if you want to accept any. Intuition tells me this will fetch us a tidy sum."

Looking away, Julia thought hard. Perhaps her emotional response to the painting will die down after a few days and she'll be able to part with it when the time comes. And, if Irene was correct and the painting secured a decent offer, then maybe she'd be able to ditch the photography for a month or two and concentrate solely on her painting. That had been her real aim all along. What if her 'pharaoh' allowed her that luxury? The idea couldn't be dismissed.

"Sounds fair enough," Julia conceded after another moment's hesitation. "If I can vet the buyer, and it's the right price, I don't see why I should withhold it from the show."

"Good. Now, I want you to get cracking on a few more like this."

Irene's grin became so broad Julia knew she was joking.

"Seriously though, just one more like this and you'll make yourself a very big name as an artist."

With a dubious look, Julia grabbed a couple of wine glasses and the corkscrew. "I don't know if that's even possible – but I'll try."

"Great."

After dinner they shared a pot of espresso and discussed the possibility of another portrait, perhaps of one of the famous Egyptian queens.

Despite the heavy dose of caffeine, Julia's eyes watered as she yawned for the third time in as many minutes. "Pardon me," she murmured.

Gathering her handbag, Irene stood. "I'd best leave you to your painting. Although, you might want to get some sleep first, your dark circles have dark circles of their own. Have you taken a look in the mirror lately?"

Julia laughed. She knew exactly what she looked like – someone who'd spent the past few days in a creative frenzy. "A nice long bath and a good night's sleep and I'll be fine."

"I'll call you," Irene promised as she waved farewell. "And don't forget – think Nefertiti."

Two

The watcher slouched lower on the bench as soon as he saw Irene exit the building. His eyes flicked up to the second floor to see the familiar play of Julia's silhouette as it reflected on the blinds, then he turned his eyes back to the BMW as it started up.

Good. She's gone. Interfering bitch.

He hated it when people visited. It made it more difficult to keep watch, though it'd been a long time since he'd had to worry about male callers. Anger welled in his chest as he contemplated that thought, but thankfully, with the exception of her idiot brother, no man had crossed her threshold since she'd settled in Boston.

At least, none he'd seen – and he'd kept a very close guard.

As he watched, one by one, the lights went out. Her bedroom, always the last, stayed on for a further ten minutes, before it, too, went dark.

Making his way back to his car, he gunned the engine with a smile – he could rest easy tonight.

He headed for the house where the meeting had been scheduled. He was late, but he didn't give a stuff. He wasn't all that sure about séances and psychic shit but he supposed it wouldn't hurt. And if it gave him the means to have power over her, without her suspecting – well why not?

How the clairvoyant woman had found him he didn't know. She said on the phone she'd seen him in a vision ... but the suspicious side of his nature wanted to deny it. Perhaps it was some kind of trap – although she'd suggested he bring a friend along if he felt uncomfortable, so he supposed she was on the up and up.

As he pulled up outside the old house a small shiver snaked up his spine. It looked ramshackle, the yard unkempt. He wondered whether he should simply turn around and go back to watching Julia's apartment, but the moment he'd thought it the front door opened to reveal an attractive woman in her middle thirties who smiled broadly at him. She wore a brightly colored scarf which covered her hair and a matching loose shift that brushed the ground. Her feet were bare.

She certainly looked the part.

"We've been waiting for you," she called, her voice softly accented, though where the accent originated, he couldn't quite tell.

"Uh, sorry," he replied sheepishly. "Took a wrong turn."

She threw him a questioning frown before gesturing he come inside, and he suddenly feared she'd caught the lie. If she could read minds ... well, he didn't want to think about it.

"That's okay," she said, her lush mouth forming another reassuring smile. "Welcome. Your friend is already here."

He found himself climbing the stairs and as he brushed by her, the woman's scent flooded his nostrils, reminding him why he'd agreed to come tonight. Julia was his. He needed an advantage, power. *I will control her.*

A dim hall opened out into a broad, windowless parlor with a large round table in the center. Candles burned brightly on every available surface, and the smell of wax and incense nauseated him.

Four people sat around the table on mismatched chairs. His friend grinned as he claimed his place alongside a stout young man who seemed Arabic in appearance.

"No names," the woman warned as she swept into the room, greeting everyone in turn by staring at each with a penetrating expression.

When her gaze came to rest directly on him it struck him that she must have partaken of some kind of drug, her eyes were overly bright and he could barely make out their color, her pupils were so large. And the waxy smoke in the air smelled vaguely of hooch. No matter. He could do it stoned. They say the oracles of ancient Greece were always off their faces and if this woman was legit, then she'd probably use any tool at her disposal.

"Are we ready?" she asked.

The Arabic man seemed hesitant. "What exactly are we going to do ... why are we here?" he asked in a low voice. "I still don't understand why you wanted me to come tonight. I don't believe in this mumbo jumbo."

The clairvoyant tilted her head to the side before answering. "You don't need to believe – but ultimately you will. You've been drawn together by forces from the great beyond. And though most of you don't yet know each other, your lives are connected. There is a task you must complete. In this you each have a role. This séance will allow the power that connects you to ignite.

"So, are we ready?" she repeated.

When nobody tried to leave, she smiled, her lips glistening in the candlelight.

Unlike the movies, the woman didn't go into a trance or speak in tongues. After several awkward minutes where they all held hands, she looked into his eyes and said: "If you want your heart's desire you'll need to join forces with those here and work together toward your goal. The forces are aligning. The spirit is restless and needs vengeance. He is so old and he has waited too long. Even now, he works in the ether to create the conditions for victory.

"Take a deep, deep breath, each of you. Count to five in your mind and then let it slowly ease out. Yes. Align your breathing, align your energies. Each of you is connected and each of you has a role to play. The rewards will be great.

"Take another deep breath and stare at the candle. Watch the flame rise."

Even though there was no wind in the room, the flame rose at her command. He shifted in his chair. *This is serious shit!*

"Breathe again," she murmured in a low voice. "Breathe part of the spirit into you – let it guide you."

Again the flame rose. Higher this time. Sweat broke out on his forehead and as he chanced a look around the table, hew saw the others were having the same reaction. He wanted to let go of the hands that held his but his fingers were paralyzed. Nothing in the room moved except the flame.

Inside, his heart raced at an alarming rate.

"Once more," she cooed. "Deeper now."

Although he wanted to fight it, the urge to do as she said was so strong he found himself obeying. Then, as his lungs reached their capacity, a sudden, sharp burn slashed across his chest like he'd been stabbed in the solar plexus. At the same instant, the flame rose and then jumped before snuffing itself out.

He tried to catch his breath. "What crap is this?" he growled as the pain reached fever pitch.

He wrenched his hands from those he held and clutched his chest, letting out a loud groan. Several of the others moaned as well, and as he lifted his eyes it became apparent he wasn't the only one to feel the imaginary blade.

"What have you done to us!"

"Be calm," the woman said. "The discomfort will pass. The spirit needed to attach to each of you ... so it could give you all the help you need. It is done."

"But what does that mean?" The Arab man surged from his chair. "Am I possessed?"

She merely smiled and went to put on the lights.

"Possession is not a word I like to use. Besides, the entity cannot take over your thoughts. It merely supports. You have taken in a fragment, if you will – a small piece of a soul that has great power. Come," she directed their attention to an arched entry that led to a sitting room scattered with couches. "I'll open a bottle of wine and we can discuss it."

*

Seth stared down at the contents of the small lacquered gift box trying to stifle his sense of dismay. The offending article had arrived a few minutes earlier by special delivery. He didn't think it odd since his birthday had been only last week but when he looked inside his gut was gripped by an intense coldness he'd never before experienced.

"What is it this time?" Rick asked as he breezed into the room without bothering to knock.

"Our friend has changed his tactics." Seth said with an air of gloom as he pushed the box across the desk with his pencil.

Rick viewed the contents without uttering a word, before he glancing up to meet Seth's eyes.

"It appears he is upping the stakes."

Seth didn't respond. Inside the box, plain for all to see was a printed card that simply said 'I can get as close as I want'. Coiled beneath the card sat a pair of antique cufflinks and a lock of Seth's hair. He knew the instant he opened the box that the hair was indeed his ... he'd noted several strands of cut hair on his pillow only few days ago and wondered how they'd gotten there.

Rick looked pointedly at Seth's hair.

"You can test – but I reckon it's mine," he said in answer to the unasked question. "And the cufflinks were a gift from my mother when I graduated college. Last time I saw them they were in my closet drawer."

"It is quite obvious that whoever he is, he's had access to your apartment. We'll need to change the locks and security codes again, and have the management scrutinize all the staff. More carefully than last time."

Seth merely nodded. Until now he'd been able to laugh off the threatening letters, but if the man, or indeed woman, had gained entrance to his apartment, he knew he had to take this threat more seriously.

"Now are you willing to have that 24 hour security team on hand to watch your back?" Rick asked with a distinct 'I told you so' expression.

"Not yet," Seth said slowly. "The one man you have at a distance is enough for now if we get those locks changed. We'll have to do the office again as well."

"But Seth, you can't–"

"Like I said before," Seth interrupted tiredly, "I cannot live with all those people hanging around me. I'll be fine–I'm not defenseless ... I do have a black belt in Judo."

"Judo is all good and well but it'll be no help against a bullet."

For the first time Seth saw the depth of Rick's unease over this. The cufflinks and hair had made the threats a whole lot more personal and it appeared Rick had decided this latest 'delivery' meant a great deal more than the letters had.

"Perhaps not, but I'll take my chances for now." He reached back and untied his hair ... then grasped a number of strands and pulled. Placing the hair in an envelope he smiled at Rick. "For your test."

*

The girl stared down the long hall lit with tiny lamps of oil. At the far end, Pharoah stood talking with his vizier. Suddenly, Pharaoh looked up and saw her. She felt as if he touched her ... and as he mouthed the word 'soon' she shivered right down to her marrow ...

The sheets were damp when Julia finally managed to extricate herself from the tangle of bedclothes. She stumbled out into the kitchen, ran herself a cool glass of water then groped around in the dark for a packet of aspirin. Her period was long overdue and the cramping had become almost unbearable. Not to mention the broken sleep.

Most of the time her irregular cycle didn't worry her – men hadn't figured in her life of late – not since that fateful day back home in

Sydney when she'd discovered that a stalker had been watching her every move ... probably for years. She still shuddered, remembering the rabid look in his eyes when she'd stepped from the shower and found him staring at her through her bathroom window not ten feet away. As she realized what he was doing she nearly vomited. She didn't have the breath to scream. She just stood there with her heart racing, half frozen and dripping wet, as his eyes rolled back and he grunted in ecstasy.

In that moment she suddenly recalled all those instances when she'd felt so uneasy at the strange sounds she'd heard late at night, alone, in her ground floor flat. A hollow ache filled her chest – a sense of violation so acute that she'd feared for her life. She felt icy cold and yet her skin burned. Her hands shook as they lifted to shield her nakedness.

She'd never forget that look on his face ... after ... when he stared up at her like a lover who'd just shared himself with her. Nausea gripped her gut every time the image flashed into her memory. His expression, an ecstatic mixture of lust and savage hate, would remain with her for life. He never uttered a word. But his face – the possessive look in his ugly, washed-out eyes – told her in no uncertain terms that he thought he owned her and it would only be a matter of time before he claimed her.

That night she did the only thing she could do: packed a bag and fled. It was lucky that she already had the airline ticket intending a surprise visit to her parents in The Hague. She simply walked up to the counter at the airport, changed her flight to the next available, and boarded without looking back.

She'd traveled about the States for several months until she found a place where she knew she'd be safe. South Boston, with its eclectic mix of cultures seemed so like the part of Sydney where she grew up, she'd felt like she'd finally found her home.

And as time passed the stalker's face invaded her mind less and less.

At the oddest moments she still saw flashes of his contorted face and the bile would instantly rise up her throat. Even now, as she thought about him, her hands unconsciously moved to cover herself. That image had forever tainted the idea of romance and lovemaking for her, so since settling in Boston she'd studiously avoided both.

If only her dreams didn't try to compensate!

She couldn't remember much of tonight's dream, but she knew for certain that her dreaming self was falling in love with her Egyptian. All she recalled was a mental snapshot from just before she awoke, but his parting expression where he gazed at her longingly, and the residue of feeling when she opened her eyes, were enough to tell her he was, in her fantasy at least, falling for her too.

Part of her thought it exciting and wildly romantic, and perhaps fascinating that she could create this exquisite drama while she dreamed. Yet the sane part of her mind knew it was crazy to even think in terms of falling in love with a long dead pharaoh ... or a photograph of him ...

She really needed to get out more. And she'd start tonight – at the opening of the exhibition. She'd make herself as beautiful as she could and then she'd find herself a gorgeous man and fall in lust with him. A real, live, man. Not some figment of her imagination. And maybe her aversion to men and sex could be cured – afterall, she'd escaped her stalker, so there was no real reason to keep her life on hold. Not anymore.

With that thought bracing her, Julia showered and dressed and headed out into the sunshine in search of a new hairstyle and a stunning outfit for the opening. She'd knock 'em dead by the time she'd finished.

*

The clairvoyant laid the cards out before him, a self-satisfied smile stretching her features.

"Ahh," she said as she formed the Celtic cross. "An interesting spread."

"Why? What is it?"

"All in good time," she murmured.

He didn't understand why she insisted an giving them all a reading ... he still thought it was mostly mumbo-jumbo, despite being slashed on the chest last time. His friend sported the same diagonal scar, almost like a tattoo, that throbbed and ached at the weirdest times.

"I don't have much time," he told her. "I've gotta get across town in less than an hour."

"You'll have plenty of time. I've already read for your friend, and what I see before me only confirms his reading."

He raised an eyebrow. "So, what's it say?"

"This card is you," she tapped at the card at the centre, the king of swords. "And this is our circumstance," she pointed to the one overlaying it – the upside-down six of pentacles. "This means there is something you desperately desire and you will be jealous if anyone else tries to take it."

Julia, he thought.

"The card crossing over it is your main obstruction."

She didn't need to tell him it was a man. The king of wands. "A dark-haired, noble man of power and intelligence – you will need to be cautious and smart to overcome him."

He shrugged, trying to make light of her pronouncement. He knew he had the upper hand over anyone who wanted her ... he knew her habits, her likes and dislikes, and he could snatch her anytime he desired. There was no man in her life, of that he was certain. The only reason he waited to claim her was because he wasn't quite ready. But he would be. And soon.

"This card ..."

He switched off and ignored the clairvoyant's droning as he imagined his first night with Julia. How she would kneel and beg before him. How she would take him in her mouth, swallow his manly essence and show her love for him. It was a vision he'd harbored for years, and it both frustrated and soothed him.

"... and this final card, shows us the probable outcome of your query. Hmmm," she mused with a slight frown. "one thing you must remember is that you can change your fate at any time, by simply changing your choices."

"Why do you say that? What does the final card mean?"

She paused for a long moment before looking him in the eye, her gaze narrowed as she assessed him. "The nine of swords – reversed."

"And that means?"

"Many things ... most often it can mean fear or shame, perhaps suspicion – occasionally imprisonment."

With a flick of his hand he swept the cards off the table. "It's all crap. I don't believe in this stuff." He stood so quickly the chair flipped over. "I'm outta here."

The clairvoyant stood too. "Like I said, it doesn't matter if you believe. But what I've seen here, along with the readings from the others, will help us plan what we have to do."

He raised his chin. "And what's that? You still haven't told us why you got us together."

Her smile wasn't mirthful or sweet. The fleshiness of her lips didn't seem at all sensual. "I think you will learn that very soon. Tonight, in fact. The spirits have told me that the convergence begins this evening, and if you pay attention you will understand what is at stake."

His wristwatch beeped, reminding him he had only half an hour to prepare and make his way to the gallery.

"Gotta go."

"I'll call you all in the morning so we can begin our quest."

He didn't have time to ask for details. Glancing down at the upturned chair, he considered picking it up. But then again the clairvoyant could clean up her own place.

*

"Here, fortify yourself," Irene handed Julia a glass of chardonnay. "I must say, you've cleaned up spectacularly, considering how disheveled you looked less than a week ago. Is the dress new?"

Julia's eyes sparkled with mischief as she twirled to display the emerald-colored silk sheath. "Everything's new. The dress, the hair, the shoes – even me." She stood and crossed Irene's plush office to stare out the window at the darkening sky. "I was sick of feeling so morose. I know, I know," she waved in dismissal as Irene began to speak. "I should go to the doctor to have my hormones checked. You said that last week."

"And I haven't changed my mind. Either do that, or find yourself a hunk and let nature take care of it – always works for me." Irene's grin became positively wicked.

"Maybe, but give me a little time, okay? I've just gotten through a horrendous month working non-stop and I plan to sit back and rest awhile." She didn't dare give Irene the satisfaction to know she intended exactly what Irene'd just suggested. Irene would never let her hear the end of it. Besides, she'd be far subtler about it – strutting her stuff with a boy-toy in tow wasn't Julia's style at all.

"All right, I'll leave you alone ... for now. But if I don't see more of those smiles soon, I'll do something drastic – like find a man for you myself."

Turning sharply, Julia glared back at her well-meaning friend. "Don't even think about it! Last time you tried that, the poor guy was gay. Very embarrassing."

Irene chose not react, they'd had this discussion before and she really felt no remorse. The man in question appeared so sexy, no one would have pegged him for being gay. Not even her, and she usually recognized the ACs from the DCs without any trouble at all; in her business she needed to be careful not to offend, whether dealing with artists or buyers – they were all somewhat temperamental.

"C'mon, Jules. It's getting near that time when we've got to go out and schmooze." Irene checked her hair and lipstick in the elaborate mirror on the back of the door, before she flung it open and headed through a short alley and into the rear entrance of the gallery. Inside waiters dashed about, putting finishing touches to the hors d'ouvrés, canapés and delicate little petit fours.

Julia drew up behind as Irene started fussing with plates and wine glasses.

When she turned, her breath died in her throat ... somehow Irene had managed to frame her pharaoh, and the portrait took pride of place on a false black wall at the very centre of the main gallery. Lights had been placed to draw the eye as soon as the viewer ventured beyond the foyer. Tears welled in her eyes – emotions she didn't know existed surged through her, threatening to overflow. Irene had taken her painting and made it the centerpiece of the show.

"Are you sure you have enough glasses?" Irene said to the nearest girl, who nodded with a slight grimace and Julia knew Irene had probably been badgering the poor waiter all afternoon. Irene rarely showed any nerves, but tonight a lot hung on the line. Apart from Julia's work, Irene was also introducing a couple of young, thus far undiscovered, artists. She had no 'big name' as a draw card. A real gamble. She'd invited the usual critics and journalists, but would the buyers and collectors come? Would they buy? – *the* million-dollar question.

"Five minutes, everyone!" Irene called out, although few of the waiters or ushers needed to be told. A massive clock, made from a combination of space age alloys and antique train parts, took pride of place in the center of the foyer; its minute hand, an electric blue arrow that changed tone in differing light, clicked loudly as it moved. "Places please!"

Several waiters moved off in the direction of the main gallery, while two ushers in black tuxedos stationed themselves next to the front door, taking up catalogues ready to hand to the visitors.

Gerry van der Gelder, Irene's long suffering assistant, cast Julia a curious smile before he unlocked the doors and swung both open as the first of the journalists reached the top step.

"Good evening, Mr Camenson," Gerry greeted, then directed his attention to the man's wife, "Mrs Camenson. Please, enjoy the excellent chablis we have tonight," he motioned toward the waiter standing just inside the doorway. He was already turning to the next guest as the Camensons strode by.

Julia wished she could hide. This was the part she hated: feeling like she was on display rather than her work, listening to the polite compliments and wondering in the back of her mind if these people really thought her work as impressive as they claimed. Without being aware she did so, she edged backward until she stood at the far end of the gallery, hidden by shadows, nursing a glass of wine she didn't dare drink.

As it turned out, the room became crowded very quickly and she felt less self-conscious, especially after overhearing some of the comments about her Egyptian portrait. She still felt of two minds whether or not to sell, but it gratified her to think others perceived the magnetism of the character she'd captured.

At about 9:30, just as the party began to wind down, a group of men approached the portrait, men she'd never seen before. After speaking with them Irene raced over to Julia, her eyes afire with excitement.

"You wouldn't believe it, Jules. See those men?" she gestured tactfully at the same group of men Julia had just spotted. "They're from the Egyptian exhibit at the Museum of Fine Arts where you took the picture."

Julia's cheeks began to burn. If they found out she'd taken the photograph, she could be charged! "God, no," she murmured. "I think I'd better make a discreet exit."

Irene stayed her movement. "Where are you going? They want to make an offer for the painting."

Julia shook her head. "No. If they realize it came from a photograph, an illegal photograph, they could have me arrested or something."

"Oh, posh! They can't prove anything. Now wait here while I do some a-grade schmoozing."

Before Julia could stop her, Irene ducked away and began making her way to the group of suited men. There were four, in all. The tallest, whose long dark hair was tied at his nape in a neat ponytail, rested his right arm in a black sling that matched his jacket. He stood with his back to her but seemed, from his easy stance and casual movements, to be fairly young, while the other three were shorter and stouter, and two were definitely a good deal older.

Scant seconds later, an exotic-looking young woman dressed in a heavily embroidered, Chinese qi pau of glowing red, joined them, and from the proprietary way she laid her hand on the tall man's uninjured arm, Julia guessed they were a couple. Her blue/black hair was twisted in one of those fashionable but untidy knots atop her head and when she turned, her pale skin, sharp features and thin lips, struck a chord deep within Julia. Had she met the woman somewhere?

As Julia watched, Irene approached the group and turned on the charm ... dazzling each man with her smile and charisma. Ever so smoothly, she touched their arms or wrists, creating an air of intimacy. Julia envied that sophistication which only Irene could exude. Before too long her agent had them all laughing and eating out of her perfectly manicured hand. All except the young woman, whose rigid stance showed she wasn't in the least impressed.

Once it appeared that Irene had things under control, Julia allowed herself to relax – the police weren't likely to drag her off yet. She took a sip of the now warm wine, and settled back against the wall to observe as the last few buyers and critics surveyed the show. Just as she was beginning to think she might slip out unnoticed, Irene pointed to her and the tall man with the ponytail turned her way.

Her breath caught.

The first thing that struck Julia was his eyes – almost leonine, they were a dark gold and felt hauntingly familiar as they pinned her with a piercing gaze. She shook off the feeling as quickly as it arose. Whoever he was, she knew she'd never met him before. If she had, she'd most certainly have remembered. She noted the hint of a bruise under his left eye. Coupled with the sling, she couldn't help but wonder if he was some kind of hired 'muscle'. The man turned away again and said something outrageous to Irene because her face became a mask of sheer dumbfoundedness – and for as long as she'd known her, Julia had never seen that look on Irene's face before.

Dear God, had they decided to have her charged over the photograph, after all?

After speaking quickly and nodding several times, Irene began to make her way toward Julia. Uh-oh, Julia thought, too late to escape now.

"You'll never guess!" Irene burst out in a loud whisper – then pulled Julia further aside so nobody could hear the next part of her revelation. "The man just offered a hundred thousand dollars for the portrait!"

The blood halted in Julia's veins for an instant before logic kicked in. "You must have misheard, Irene. That's ridiculous."

Irene shook her head, over and over, as if she couldn't believe it herself. "He said one hundred grand. Twice. I nearly asked him to say it a third time just to be sure, but I realized I'd sound like an absolute idiot. I told him the artist wasn't decided about selling, so he sent me over to ask you."

Julia spun about until she faced the wall, not knowing whether to laugh or cry or squeal ... or what! A hundred thousand dollars would allow her to give up the commercial photography and stick to what she loved best.

But ... but ... there must be a catch ...

She spun back. "Why would he make such an exorbitant offer? It doesn't make any sense at all." She glanced up and noticed the man continued to watch her. Her heart skipped a little. "Why?" she whispered, almost to herself.

"Who cares why, Jules? This will make you as an artist. Once everyone hears that one of your pieces sold for three figures, they'll clamor for your work. This could be your big break. Come on, let's go over and tell them you'll sell." Irene grabbed her arm and started pulling her along.

"No, Irene," she shook her off and backed up a step. "I don't know. This doesn't make any sense at all. Maybe there's a catch."

"What do you mean? The man has lots of money and wants to give you a great deal of it in exchange for a painting of one of his ancestors. What sort of catch can there be?"

Julia's face shot up. "Ancestors? Did he say that, Irene? Did he say it was one of his ancestors?" A shiver ran over Julia's shoulders and down her spine, setting every fine hair on her body to attention.

Irene scowled. "Something like that. What of it? Who the hell cares why he wants it? So long as his money's good, I'm not going to argue." Again she grasped Julia's arm and tried to drag her forward, but Julia stood her ground.

A strange sensation flooded her chest. It wasn't fear, exactly. Nor was it excitement. It was something in between, a feeling that filled her with both elation and dread. A prescient feeling that seemed to touch her very marrow. This man meant something, just as the painting did – just as the exhibition at the museum did. Just as her dreams did.

He stared at her openly. Julia could feel it in the very same way she'd known the photograph stared at her when she'd developed it. Her fingers shook as she shielded her eyes with her hand and tried to think. Maybe her hormones were so out of balance that her imagination was running wild. She took several deep breaths, trying to let cold reason take control. Yes, that was it. Just like in her dreams, her imagination was getting the better of her. She'd been working too hard, alone too long.

She just needed to step back, to take stock and all this nonsense would simply disappear.

A hundred thousand dollars.

She raised her eyes slowly. "Irene—" She didn't get to say more, her breath deserted her instead. While she'd been attempting to regain her composure, the man with the ponytail had approached and now stood directly before her. Her pulse-rate soared the moment their eyes met.

"Julia," Irene said, "I'd like you to meet Seth Almose, the banker here in Boston who co-sponsored the recent Egyptian exhibit at the Museum of Modern Art." She turned to Seth. "Seth, this is the artist, Julia Morrow."

As his amber eyes traveled over Julia's features, it felt as if he'd stripped away every ounce of make-up she wore and saw the real woman beneath. The look made her want to shiver and again the sensation that she knew him flashed across her mind. Yet at the same time she knew without doubt, she'd never laid eyes on him.

"Ms Morrow." He said her name in soft rich tones, a caress, laced with the trace of an accent that she couldn't quite place. "I'm very impressed with your painting." He reached across with his free hand and took hers, raising it so he could brush a gentle kiss on her knuckles.

Her fingers tingled.

His eyes again caught hers and she saw an implacable determination rising within them. "I mean to purchase it for my office."

She smiled weakly and extricated her hand as she attempted to find her voice. "Thank you for your kind words ... but as I said to Irene, I'm not sure I want to sell that particular painting. Would you mind if I think it over?"

Seth appeared to breathe deeply and draw himself up to his full height, which dwarfed her by more than a foot. His eyes shone and the corners of his lips lifted ever so slightly. "I can wait, Ms Morrow. I've waited a very long time."

With those enigmatic words, he nodded to Irene, handed her his business card and started toward the foyer to meet his companions. At the very last minute, his gaze flicked back to Julia and he mouthed the word 'soon' as he exited.

This time Julia didn't suppress the shiver. In fact, she welcomed it. It was a real and physical sensation. The whole confrontation seemed almost surreal. What on earth did he mean by 'soon'? Where had she seen that exact scene before?

"Whew!" Irene muttered, fanning herself as if overwhelmed by a hot flush. "Was he not the sexiest man you've ever come across? My advice, Jules, is to go for it!"

With a shake of her head, Julia glared at her friend. "What are you talking about?"

"Ha! What am I talking about?" Irene tsk-tsked. "Julia, Julia. The man literally devoured you with his eyes – more's the pity," her voice seethed with envy, "I reckon all you have to do is say the word and he's yours for the taking."

Julia felt herself choking as Irene's words sank in. "Do you ever think of anything but sex?"

Irene frowned. "Money often invades my mind, too. Seriously, Jules, the air around you both sizzled. Didn't you sense it? Surely–"

Holding up her hand to cut Irene off, Julia turned her face away. She took several slow breaths then turned back, trying to hide her grimace behind a smile. "Irene, I really don't know..." What didn't she know? All she did know was his offer staggered her and she couldn't think straight. "Look, we're all very tired and I think it best if I just head on home."

"But what about the painting, are you going to sell, or not?" Irene asked, tapping Seth's card against her palm and, Julia suspected, calculating her commission. "I'll need to give Mr Almose a call and let him know. Shall I give him your number if he asks?"

Sighing, Julia closed her eyes and shook her head. "No – don't. Let me have a few days. I need sleep and some time on my own before I decide what to do about Mr Almose."

"But didn't we agree, not three hours ago, that being alone is what you didn't need?"

"Let it go, Irene. A few days isn't going to make much difference. This is a very big decision for me. It could change my life in a lot of ways."

"Why?" Irene asked as if dismayed. "You only need to sleep with the man, not marry him."

"Dammit, Irene, I wasn't even talking about that! I'm talking about the painting." She turned again, determined to go before she and Irene ended up arguing. "I'll call you on Monday, okay? I'll have an answer about the painting then."

Irene shrugged. "If that's what you want."

"Yeah, it's exactly what I want."

*

In a dark niche, the watcher maintained his vigil. He'd kept one eye on her all evening and now it had drawn to a close he watched her walk out the door. Anger and lust warred within him, compelling him to move. To follow. But he had to take care of other business first – in exchange for admission to tonight's opening, he'd promised to help pack up. His friend had proved invaluable – he was legitimately closer to her, so he couldn't renege no matter how much he wanted to just up and leave.

In the past every time he'd begun to get close, he'd worried that she'd remember. Not this time though. He taken great pains to develop a convincing American accent and his new hair color, contacts, moustache and trendy clothes completed the transformation. At one point tonight she'd stared straight at his face and hadn't recognized him. That was gratifying – it meant he could be more open in his movements. Only time would tell.

He grinned to himself. He was content to wait until he had all his plans in place – and if they fell in with another's designs, so much the better. For too long, he'd waited. For too long, she'd denied him his reward. And he wasn't about to have her slip through his fingers again. It had taken him months to locate her – shadowing her brother half way across Australia then to Holland, before the fool finally came to Boston to deliver the noisy parrot she doted upon. He'd watched her in the park 'walking' the stupid creature – she showered it with affection – affection that rightly belonged only to him. Well that lump of feathers would be the first to go now he had her right where he wanted her. All he needed to do was make sure she stayed put.

Later.

Later tonight, after more immediate concerns were done with – he'd follow then. Julia was his alone and she'd learn that very soon.

The thought of how he'd teach her sent a delicious bolt of desire through his gut. He felt his body harden. With a casual nonchalance he brushed his hand over his groin, impressed by his own prowess – by the power that lay hidden there. Yes. Soon.

As he turned to begin collecting wine glasses, he frowned – he'd have to keep tabs on that banker, though. He didn't like the way the man had looked at Julia. Not at all.

And he intended to confront the clairvoyant. He'd been barely able to hide his surprise when he saw her strolling around the gallery like she belonged – talking to other guests as if she was one of them. She looked nothing like she had only an hour before ... but her eyes were unmistakable.

How she'd known where they'd be, he couldn't begin to understand. For the most part she'd ignored him, but when their paths crossed at one point, she'd winked at him. She was either following him, or was an incredibly talented psychic. The cynic in him assumed the former ... but if she really was clairvoyant, perhaps he could make better use of her. He'd barely paid attention to the reading she'd given him earlier. *Maybe I'll get her to do it again. A deeper reading. And if I can steal something of Julia's, I could give it to the clairvoyant and get her to tell me when and how to make my move.*

*

The split down the side of Hannah's dress revealed the length of her shapely thigh as she shifted on the white leather seat of the limousine. It was a deliberate move, and Seth knew it. She slid her hand closer, brushing his hip as the car turned a corner.

"*Hannah.*" He said her name like a warning.

Turning her warm chocolate gaze upon him, she raised her chin in defiant innocence. "Hmm?"

With any other woman, he knew he'd probably feel flattered, but Hannah's obsessive pursuit had become an irritant in recent weeks.

"It's been over for a long time."

She leaned toward him, her tongue darting out to moisten her lower lip. Another calculated action. "It doesn't have to be," she cooed. "Just say the word and I'll come home with you. It could be like it used to be for us."

"Like it used to be? There never really was any 'us.'"

"That's because you never gave us a chance."

Seth shook his head almost sadly. "You know it wouldn't work, Hannah. And you know why."

Rolling her eyes, she looked away. "That precious curse of yours." For a second she sagged back in the seat before she turned and sneered. "How do you know I'm not the one? Hmm?"

With a tired sigh, Seth stared out at the blur of lights as the limousine sped along. "Like I told you over a year ago, I just know." He laid his head back against the headrest and let his eyes drift closed, wondering how many women he'd have to say it to before he found the one he searched for.

Celine was another. With her he'd also hoped and it pained him to remember that night in San Francisco when he'd ended it with her.

It astounded him when Celine turned up on his doorstep a few months ago acting as though their final confrontation was a mere misunderstanding. He'd been cordial but had let her know in no uncertain terms that there was no chance they would rekindle the relationship.

He was jarred from his memories by Hannah's hand insinuating itself onto his lap.

Quick as lightning, he lifted it away again, squeezing her wrist firmly. He didn't want to hurt her but enough was enough!

"I'm not going to tell you again, Hannah. It's not going to happen. If you won't be content with friendship, then we can't even see each other on a social level."

Hannah pouted. "She's not the one, you know."

Seth's brow knitted into a deep frown. "Who?"

"That painter – the one who did that portrait. I saw how you ogled her. It was written all over your face – as soon as you saw that picture you were thinking you'd found the woman of your precious curse."

Glancing at the tinted window, he grimaced at his own reflection. "The thought never entered my head," he lied.

"No?" Hannah laughed. "Then why'd you offer so much money for such an awful painting?"

The heated look Seth shot her should have melted the make-up from her face. "How I spend my money is my own business. And, despite what you think, I believe that painting is an excellent investment. Mr Ewing, the appraiser who accompanied us tonight, concurred wholeheartedly."

Hannah snorted but said nothing more until the car came to a stop outside her apartment block. "Are you sure you won't come in? We could just sit and talk – if that's all you want." She reached out her hand but Seth gently blocked the movement.

"Please, Hannah, I'm tired of this game."

"It's not a game."

"No?" he raised an eyebrow.

She shook her head and affected a tearful expression. She'd done that before, too – on more than one occasion.

"Don't bother with the waterworks – that wore off after the first couple of attempts. Go on home." He gave a weary sigh.

"Fine," she snapped, her mood and countenance changing like she'd flicked a switch. "But you'll regret letting me go. Of that, I promise you."

Seth schooled his features as he tried not to laugh at her ridiculous threat.

The driver opened the door, then stood aside and waited.

"Just go home, Hannah," Seth repeated.

For long seconds she stared at him, her face a mask of utter indignation, before she turned away. She didn't even deign to say goodnight.

Elegant to the last, she allowed the driver to hand her out of the car and escort her to the lobby.

Not once did she look back.

Seth was thankful her ploy hadn't erupted into a major scene. He just hoped that she'd finally take him at his word.

And he'd have a great deal to say to his meddling cousin, come Monday. Jamal should never have invited Hannah along if he didn't intend to escort her home. He didn't know whether it was Hannah's idea or Jamal's, but it was the last time he'd be suckered into being alone with her. Next time, Jamal could call her a cab.

As the driver started the car, Seth rubbed the knuckles of his injured hand. They still ached, but they were definitely getting better.

Three

Julia returned to a silent apartment. Bird sat sleeping on his perch and the room appeared almost naked without her canvasses spread about. Only one remained, leaning like an abandoned waif against the far wall, but she hadn't yet done anything more than sketch basic outlines.

Exhaustion swept over her. She barely had the energy to remove her gown and shoes before she stumbled into bed.

"Mmmm!" she groaned, her eyes drifting closed the instant she smelled the familiar lavender fragrance of her sheets.

Seth Almose's face sprang into her mind the moment her eyes shut, but she felt so drained, she didn't have the wherewithal to push it away. On a sigh, she let him follow her as she slipped back into her dream . . .

Pharaoh stood before her, tall and strong, adorned in his gold and blue head dress, his amber eyes kohled. For long seconds he just looked down at her with an almost perplexed gaze, then slowly, he lowered his head and touched her lips with his. A mixture of excitement and terror swelled in her breast. She was just an enslaved princess, he was king and god ...

Julia sat bolt upright and shook. That was where she'd seen those eyes. Her dreams. Her silly, nonsensical dreams! The man in her dreams – the pharaoh on her corkboard – had kissed her. But in her dream that stone face had become quite real and he looked identical to Seth. Was that why he'd seemed so familiar? Or had she just taken Seth Almose's face and placed it in the dream so she could somehow make it more real? She was certain she hadn't met Seth prior to last night. Had she already met him in her dreams?

She scrubbed her face, rubbing the sleep from her eyes, then slumped back against her pillow. "Oh, God – now I know I'm losing my mind."

Light had just begun to filter through her translucent lace curtains and a glance at the clock told her it was a little after six. She hadn't had nearly enough sleep, but, now that she was awake, she felt wide awake. And she knew it would serve no purpose to stay in bed going over and over what little she recalled from her dream, or the events of last night. Better instead to be up and about and doing things.

After a quick shower, Julia threw on some old sweats and left her apartment with the intention of walking to the nearby patisserie to buy fresh croissants for breakfast. Whether she agreed to sell the painting or not, she could at least treat herself like she would have done if the exhibition had been a success. And now, as she thought about it, she realized it was a success. A big success. Even if she didn't sell her Egyptian portrait, she'd still make a tidy sum from the other works sold.

The street was tranquil at this time of morning. A few cars passed, or the occasional truck, but for the most part she walked alone in the early morning freshness.

"Thanks, Artie." She smiled at the pastry chef as he handed her the warm croissant wrapped in a napkin and a foam cup of steaming tea. Instead of heading home, she decided to walk around the block and enjoy the peace. Her neighborhood had wonderful old character houses and big leafy trees, but in an hour or two, it would transform as the world came alive; the traffic would be heavy and there'd be the tourists as well as the locals, all so involved in the rapid comings and goings of daily life, they barely took the time to stop and notice the beauty that surrounded them.

As she crossed the street so she could walk along the side of the park, a prickling of her skin told Julia she was no longer alone. A tall man, dressed in black, jogged directly toward her and being so early in the morning, with not another soul in sight, memories of her stalker suddenly loomed large in her mind.

Her heart began to race.

Would she ever be free of him?

She knew she'd appear quite ridiculous if she crossed over again in order to avoid him, so in spite of her fear she bit down on her croissant, increased her pace and stared straight at him to show she wasn't in the least intimidated.

As he drew rapidly closer, it struck her that the man approaching wasn't some stranger – no, that wasn't exactly true – he was a stranger, but she had met him. Only last night. His tall frame and long ponytail were unmistakable.

The jogger was Seth Almose, minus the sling.

He raised a hand in salute and slowed his stride.

"Good morning, Ms Morrow," he greeted as he halted before her. "I'm surprised to see you up and about so early, especially after such a big evening."

She sipped her tea before speaking. "I'd normally be out to it – but for some odd reason I couldn't seem to sleep."

A dark brow lifted. "Not bad dreams, I hope."

Julia's breath caught for just an instant. Was the man psychic? She looked him in the eye, but his face belied no hint of prescience.

"No, not bad dreams." If only he'd known. The dream, what little she recalled, wasn't bad at all. In fact, if she was honest she admit liked it. A lot. She was still at a loss to know whether she'd dreamed about Seth at other times, or whether she'd injected his face into the dream after last night's encounter, but the question was really neither here nor there, since it was, after all, just a dream. A fiction.

Though the kiss had seemed so very real. Her lips tingled, even now.

Seth smiled and his golden irises seemed to catch fire in the early morning light. "That's good to hear. My ancestors believed that dreams were omens. Or memories of some wrong in the past which needs to be righted."

A small flutter flashed through her belly. For just a moment she thought she remembered something else but she pushed it away before the memory could properly form. She didn't want or need such nonsense.

"And you, Mr Almose, do you believe dreams are omens?" she said, deliberately trying to sound cynical.

He slanted her a sideways look. "Perhaps – I'm sure I'll learn the answer some time soon.

"Tell me, Ms Morrow, is that pastry as delicious as it smells?"

She glanced down at her half-eaten croissant and laughed. "Better. Do you want one?"

He nodded. "Show me where I can buy some."

Julia pointed to the adjoining street.

"Pierre's."

She led him around the corner to the patisserie and waited while he went inside. Moments later, when he emerged with a big sack and a steaming cup of coffee, they sat alongside each other on the concrete stoop of the shop next door.

"You're right, Ms Morrow," he said after he'd eaten two of the buttery croissants.

"Julia, please," she offered, unable to prevent a smile. "And what am I right about?"

"They are better than they smell. Superb." He peeked into the bag again, then offered her a delicate *cat's tongue* – "'Dessert,'" he explained.

"Thanks, but I don't really eat much for breakfast."

"Ah, but Julia, they are small," he took a bite of one and gazed at her for a long second, "and exquisite."

She shook her head.

"'Tis your loss and my gain," he gave her a roguish grin then swallowed another, whole.

"Be careful, Mr Almose, you'll get fat, that is, of course, if you don't choke first."

"You must call me Seth, Julia. And I promise not to choke ... or get fat."

Their eyes met and held for another long moment and she knew he spoke the truth about the latter. His physique was one that could only come from spending a reasonable amount of time in a gym or on some training track. And his rich black hair shone brightly in the sun. Oh yes, he definitely took care of himself.

She glanced up and realized that he was assessing her, too.

They both laughed – a knowing, yet slightly nervous laugh that acknowledged each recognized the subtle energy that had begun to pass between them.

"Well," she said as she stood, "I guess I'd better be getting back and do some work."

"You work on Saturday? Is there no place in your life for rest and entertainment?"

Tilting her head, she thought for a moment. Recently, there honestly hadn't been and she supposed it'd become habit to spend almost all her waking hours painting, or processing film.

"I get plenty of time for entertainment," she lied. "But, right now I'm working on a series I want to get finished." *Where had that come from?* Yet, even as she thought about it, she knew she'd spoken the truth. She'd only just begun to explore this Egyptian theme. Her dream last night, despite Seth's presence in it, made her feel as if there was so much more about her pharaoh buried inside her, which she'd eventually have to get down onto canvas.

Seth broke into her distracted musing. "Could you not spare a few hours later to join me for lunch? I will admit to having an ulterior motive—"

"Oh?" Her eyes narrowed slightly.

He grinned, his expression betraying a kind of boyish mischief. "The museum is holding a small reception to celebrate the success of the Egyptian exhibit. I'll have one last chance to look upon the relics of my ancestors before they're crated and shipped back to Egypt. I'm hoping you'll accompany me."

Her face lit up. "To see the exhibition one last time?"

"Not the whole exhibit," he explained. "Just Tuthmosis's artifacts. The rest is already packed away. It is the last room and the gallery wanted to give me a private viewing since our bank acted as principal sponsor."

"I'd love to," Julia exclaimed, a sense of warmth filling her chest. "His relics, as you would already have guessed, were the inspiration for the portrait."

"And that is another thing," he added with a smile, "I wanted another opportunity to convince you to sell the painting to me."

She pressed her lips into a thin line, feigning hesitation. But underneath there wasn't a question in her mind. Whether she decided to sell the painting or not, she'd go to the luncheon with him. Anything to get another look at her pharaoh.

"Where and when?"

His smile widened and his irises dilated as he gazed down at her. "I'll pick you up at 11.45. Will that give you enough time?"

"Yes, but I can make my own way there."

"I wouldn't think of it."

She frowned at first but acquiesced with a sigh.

"I'd better give you my address."

He held up his hand to halt her, reciting the details as if he knew it well.

"How–?"

Seth shook his head. "I have my sources."

"But–"

"I must get back myself," he said before she could demand an explanation. "We can talk at lunch."

Reluctantly, she nodded. "See you at 11.45 then."

Seth turned and started back toward the park, then began a slow jog once he reached the grassy verge.

Julia watched as he grew more distant, studying the graceful way he moved, so effortless and streamlined, just like the pharaoh in her dream, the pharaoh who now wore Seth's face.

Oh God, I'm becoming obsessed!

Maybe she shouldn't go back and take another look – perhaps it'd only exacerbate the preoccupation. No, that was ridiculous – she was just tired from lack of sleep and all the excitement over the successful showing at Irene's gallery. She'd go home, have a bubble bath and pamper herself. She'd accompany Seth to take a last look at her pharaoh – then she'd say goodbye, to both the man and the pharaoh, and go back to painting her landscapes.

And there was always another wedding shoot waiting to be printed.

*

At exactly 11.45 the doorbell chimed. Julia inspected herself in the hall mirror before heading for the front door. She'd chosen to wear a soft green outfit that highlighted her eyes – the skirt skimmed the top of her knees but was, at the same time, safely businesslike. Her wheat-colored hair bounced around her shoulders in soft curls and she'd applied the barest cover of make-up. Simplicity.

Seth, in black trousers and a casual sports coat, greeted her with an appreciative glance as she held the door wide.

"Come in a minute," she suggested. "I just have to grab my purse."

Ducking back into her bedroom, she left him in the living room to meet Bird.

True to form, Bird began swearing and squawking as soon as Seth moved within range.

"Strange pet you have," he commented when she returned.

"Hmmm, isn't he? My brother gave me Bird shortly after I arrived in Boston – he thought I'd appreciate a little reminder of home. Several of his friends thought it'd be fun to teach him how to swear. Needless to say, he's been an embarrassment ever since. Haven't you, Bird?" she reached over and stroked the parrot's pink throat. Bird, in turn, curved himself into her hand until he nearly fell off his perch. "He's a real softie, too."

Unlike most of her guests, who were generally frightened of Bird's long beak and sharp claws, Seth held out his hand and stroked the bird's other side. "Yes, he is. But he seems a good companion. Can he fly?"

"Oh yes, I hate the idea of any bird's wings being clipped. Or cages. He has the run of the flat and we sometimes go to the park. He's well trained and is also a very effective watch-dog."

Seth laughed at that.

"Okay Bird, we've gotta' go. You behave yourself and I'll bring you home a treat." She leaned down and allowed Bird to preen her cheek before she straightened.

"Shall we?" he motioned that she precede him.

On the way to the museum they discussed Bird's girlfriend, a macaw who lived down the block and came to visit whenever its owner went on vacation, and the pros and cons of city living.

"How long have you painted?"

"All my life, really," she answered as he held the car door for her. "Photography is a stop-gap measure. You know, pay the bills so I could indulge myself in my painting." She stepped out onto the sidewalk and smiled her thank you.

"And how did you meet, Irene?"

"Now that is a very long story – one I might tell you some time, but right now I'd like to go and have a last look at Tuthmosis."

"A last look?" he asked, his brows rising quizzically as they strode through the foyer toward the stairs to the exhibition rooms.

For a moment Julia felt her face warm. She forgot that no one else knew of her most recent visits to the museum, and that of all the rooms in the exhibition, Tuthmosis's was the only one she'd entered. She couldn't dare tell Seth that his invitation only fed what seemed to be a sick obsession.

"I suppose, since I'm not likely to vacation in Egypt anytime soon, that it'll be a long while before I see any of his relics again," she said by way of excuse as she stepped across the threshold into the Tuthmosis room.

"Perhaps not, but you have his portrait – for now," he grinned as if to say that he'd rectify that particular problem in the very near future, "and I did happen to see the photograph–"

"Oh, no – please, if it's going to get me into trouble, I'll destroy it, and the negative."

He laughed. "Why should it get you into trouble?"

She didn't answer, rather, she indicated the very large sign that forbade photography of any kind within the exhibit.

Again he laughed. "Don't tell me you've been worried I'd have you arrested?"

She looked away. "Well ... the thought did occur to me."

Lifting her chin with his index finger, his amber gaze drove deeply into hers. "If you knew me better, you'd realize how ludicrous that idea is. But, since you don't, you'll just have to take my word that I have no interest in causing you any trouble, in fact ..."

He didn't finish; one of the attendants flicked on the main lights and for the first time Julia saw the statue of Tuthmosis without any of the special lighting effects used during the exhibition. Further, the glass casing and false pedestal were gone.

"Oh, lord," she breathed, thinking how much more captivating the statue became without the backlighting and the thick glass which held him aloof from all onlookers. The face seemed so real, the urge to reach up and touch became almost too strong to resist. "He's magnificent."

An unreadable expression crossed Seth's dark features. "Do you think so?"

Julia nodded, knowing words could not adequately describe what she felt. The pull this ancient pharaoh had upon her heightened more every moment she stared at his carved image. And now it stood naked, or so it seemed, the stark realism of the statue reached out with an intimacy that clutched at her core. It was as if she knew him, had known him eons ago, and the emotions which that sensation evoked made her shiver deep inside. Her dream of the night before sprang instantly to mind. She remembered that breath of a kiss – a gentle and fleeting touch that remained imprinted on her lips, as if the man alongside her had been the one to bestow it.

She snatched a deep lungful of air and her eyes darted up to Seth's face. He was studying her in a most peculiar way and she could almost imagine he really was the pharaoh of her dream. Could he know? Did he share the dream, perhaps?

A small bubble of laughter arose with the thought. *What utter nonsense.*

She turned back to the statue and whispered, "I wish I'd known him."

An instant later she felt Seth's warm breath brush against her cheek as he leaned closer to her ear. "Do you believe in reincarnation, Julia? An afterlife? Or fate?"

She turned sharply, hoping to read his meaning, but his expression remained benign. He stood so close she could see the darker spots of brown that speckled his golden irises. And as she watched, his pupils dilated as if drawing more than the sight of her into himself. Her heart seemed to falter yet she couldn't shift her gaze away. Deep within, she knew he wanted to kiss her, but for some reason he appeared to be waiting for something – a sign, perhaps? Her permission?

"Do you believe in reincarnation?" he repeated in a quiet whisper as he moved closer still.

"I ... I ..." she stuttered, unable to gather her thoughts. What was he doing to her? Closing her eyes, she shut out his face, a useless attempt to shake away the impression that she'd suddenly fallen headlong into her dream from the night before.

When she finally lifted her lids he no longer looked at her at all, but at the statue.

"Do you want to touch him?" Seth asked.

"Oh yes," she replied without thinking about it. "Last time I came I tried to feel him through the glass – it sounds silly, I know."

He didn't laugh at her, but took hold of her hand and splayed his like a fan over the back until each of his fingers rested between one of hers. He wound his thumb into her palm and she felt a tiny spark race from the center through to each and every nerve in her arm. Goosebumps rose over her skin.

But before she had a chance to analyze any of it, he raised their joined hands and pressed them to the statue's cheek. The stone felt icy cold compared to the heat of their hands.

"Won't we get into trouble?" she murmured urgently, though she was unable to take her eyes from their joined hands as they rested on her pharaoh's carved face.

Seth moved closer until his body molded itself behind hers and his chin rested atop her head. She sucked in a breath.

"No, we're quite alone," he murmured, "and the curator trusts me not to damage the relics of my ancestors.

"Can you feel the life in him?" he asked as he drew their joined hands slowly, almost sensuously, down the statue's cheek and throat until their fingertips found the center of Tuthmosis's chest, his heart. "There is a myth that he fell deeply in love with a slave girl and when she disappeared, he vowed to search both this world and the next, until he found her again."

Julia snatched her hand away and edged around the statue.

"Do you think it's true?"

She asked the question in order to place some emotional distance between Seth and herself. The more she learned of him, the more dangerous he became to her well-being. It had been a long time since any man elicited the reactions he'd just done, and it scared the heck out of her. The statue did too. It seemed that her feelings were beginning to be all tangled up between the dream, Seth, and the ancient pharaoh who'd worn Seth's face.

And the myth, if true, only confused her more. In the farthest reaches of her mind she recalled snippets of other dreams that seemed to hint at ... at what? A similar story? Maybe she'd read about the myth years ago when she'd studied art history. Or perhaps she'd read some reference to it in the catalogue she'd bought last time she'd attended the exhibit – and she'd woven the story into the dream just as she'd done with Seth's face?

She didn't consciously remember. But whether she'd dreamt it or read it, it didn't matter. Her obsession with Tuthmosis needed to stop right now. When she got home she'd take the photo off the wall and file it away, then get rid of all reminders of the exhibit and go back to her landscapes.

"I've decided to sell you the painting," she blurted, mentally including that in her list of items to dispose of in order to return to sanity.

"I'm glad," he murmured. Then, before she could prevent him, he drew her into his arms and touched her lips with a fleeting, but soul-binding kiss. "There," he added as he gently put her away from him, "the bargain is sealed."

Julia shook. The kiss so resembled the scene from last night's dream she began to wonder if this too was a dream. Though they were different times and different places, the occurrences seemed to merge – as if she'd developed some kind of precognition.

From behind, a waiter cleared his throat in a mock show of politeness. Julia's pulse jumped.

She backed away.

"Luncheon is served in the anteroom. If you'll follow me."

Julia turned her eyes back to the statue, a quiet feeling of emptiness swept over her at the idea of bidding farewell. Yet she knew her obsessive reactions bordered on unhealthy. In her mind, she ordered herself to let go ... after all, if she wanted contact, all she needed to do was dream. She had no control over that.

Seth held out his hand. "Come, I promised you lunch, let us see what delights the chef has prepared for us."

Without considering the consequences of again touching him, she took his hand and let herself be led through to the anteroom next door. A delicious array of seafood lay beckoning alongside a small table set for intimate dining. A single white lily sat in a slim vase between the perfectly laid place settings, and a bottle of champagne rested in a frosty bucket beside the table.

She'd assumed the reception would include a large contingent of staff from the gallery and the visiting exhibit, as well as the sponsors.

"Isn't the curator or his staff joining us?"

"No," he directed her to her chair and helped her sit, "it's just us. I hope you like seafood."

"I adore it – but didn't you say this reception was for the sponsors?"

"Indeed, it is," he confirmed as he sat in the chair opposite.

"But–"

"Lobster?" He carefully removed her plate and began to serve small pieces of succulent white meat. "Shrimp?"

She nodded.

"The bank I work for is the primary sponsor of the exhibit – apart from the British and Egyptian governments, of course."

"But what about the curator – shouldn't he be here?"

"Daniel's busy supervising the packing of the exhibit and cannot spare the time to join us. He sends his apologies, though. So I'm afraid you must endure my company for a short while longer. Will that be a hardship?"

Her eyes darted up to meet his and she immediately read mischief in their golden depths. In an instant she understood this was probably just an elaborate 'set up' he'd planned in order to persuade her to sell her painting. The very idea made her laugh.

"You find my question humorous, Julia?"

"Not at all – I just realized that I caved in too quickly, that's all."

"Caved in?"

"Yes. I should've waited until after dessert before I agreed to sell – are you terribly disappointed?"

His warm eyes sparkled as he picked up the bottle of Bollinger and poured them both a small measure. "Ah, so you think I am wining and dining you in an attempt to convince you to sell the painting. To answer your question, yes – I'm disappointed. Not because you caught me out, mind you, but because I have more honor than you credit me, as you will no doubt learn." He handed her the champagne flute and tapped his glass against hers. A rich 'ping' echoed through the room. "To fate, reincarnation and our friend Tuthmosis."

Holding her gaze captive with his, he slowly lowered his frosty glass to his lips and tasted the wine.

Julia's hand stilled as she watched his lower lip touch the glass; a frisson of adrenalin shot through her midriff. It felt as if his lip touched her, tasted her. She couldn't take her eyes off his mouth. A sinuous thread of desire seemed to wrap itself around her, robbing her of the ability to think.

When he lowered his glass, she swallowed along with him.

"Don't you like champagne?" he asked, a hint of a grin playing at the corners of his lips.

"Champagne?" Julia blinked. "Oh – yes, I love champagne, although I don't generally drink at this time of day, especially on an empty stomach."

He grinned. "Then I guess we'd better eat."

"Achem."

Both Julia and Seth turned in the same instant. A dark-suited man stood silhouetted in the open doorway. He stepped into the light.

Julia recognized his face immediately. Gerry van der Gelder worked for Irene at the gallery, and had done so for a number years. Since Irene became her agent, Julia'd met him on numerous occasions, but she couldn't honestly call him a friend. There'd always been something furtive about the way he watched her that gave Julia a distinct feeling of discomfort. Thinking logically, she couldn't quite say why; he'd never said or done anything overt, so she'd put her uneasiness down to the psychological legacy left by her stalker.

Still, afterward she always felt relieved to escape his scrutiny.

Why he'd shown up here, now, she couldn't even begin to guess.

"Excuse me for interrupting, Mr Almose," he said with a curious smile which didn't extend beyond a baring of teeth. He turned his gaze on Julia and gave a slight nod, "Julia."

"Hello, Gerry," she responded in a sober tone.

"What can I do for you, Mr ... ?" Seth raised an eyebrow.

Gerry moved closer and extended his hand to Seth, forcing him to stand. Seth was taller and broader, and altogether more masculine. Gerry appeared almost boyish and effeminate alongside.

"...van der Gelder – Gerry van der Gelder. We met at last night's opening of Irene's exhibition – which, as you no doubt know, included a number of Julia's artworks," he explained.

"Indeed. As you can see, Ms Morrow and I are enjoying a private meal – is there some reason you stopped by?" Seth words were silky and smooth, but implied an underlying impatience.

Stuttering slightly, Gerry straightened his tie. "I–ah, I needed to hand Julia a check for several pieces that sold prior to the opening. I was attending a meeting in the office upstairs when someone mentioned Julia was in the building." He pulled an envelope from his breast pocket and flourished it while he perused the sumptuous array of seafood on the table before him. "Since I'd intended delivering it to your apartment after taking lunch in the cafe downstairs, I thought I'd stop by now and save myself the trip – I hope it's okay, Julia." He stared down at her in a peculiar way and she had to quell a sudden wave of discomfort.

"Of course," she replied as she took the envelope. "Thank Irene for me."

Seth resumed his seat. "If that is all, Mr van der Gelder, Ms Morrow and I were just about to share a bottle of fine champagne. You will excuse us, won't you?"

Gerry's face slowly flushed – no doubt it rankled that he'd been dismissed so offhand. Julia wondered whether he'd hoped to be invited to join them for lunch. There was certainly enough food, but she didn't think she'd have much of an appetite if he stayed.

"Of course," Gerry said. "I do apologize for the interruption."

Julia wasn't sure, but she thought she heard Seth mutter what sounded like: "I'll just bet" under his breath.

Gerry's face belied an unguarded hardness as he walked to the door.

As soon as Gerry had gone, Seth turned to her and furrowed his brow. "There is something about that man....." he left the sentence hanging and Julia understood why. She'd never been able to put her finger on it either – yet she felt vindicated knowing that someone else experienced the same sense of unease around Gerry.

"Tell me, has he made an pass?"

Julia gaped in surprise. "Pass? D'you mean ... romantically?"

Seth flashed her a penetrating look. "It's plain the man is smitten with you."

Julia's fork slipped from her fingers and clattered to the floor.

"Gerry?" she gave a nervous little laugh and shook her head. *Absolutely preposterous!* "I don't think so. I've never liked the man, and he hasn't once given the impression he likes me. If anything, I usually sense animosity."

Seth's scrutiny intensified for a moment, before he allowed his eyes to return to the plate before him. "Perhaps," his lips thinned, "Still ..."

A waiter materialized and replaced her fork before she had a chance to bend down to retrieve it.

With an enigmatic expression Seth ordered her to eat, and it wasn't long before all thought of Gerry van der Gelder was forgotten as Seth regaled her with stories about his younger brothers and his business. Much later, the waiter discreetly began to clear the remains of their meal.

Seth leaned over the table, "I suspect he is trying to tell us something," he whispered as he motioned toward the waiter.

Glancing at her wristwatch, Julia's eyes widened. "We've been sitting here for nearly three hours – he probably has better things to do than stand here and eavesdrop while we sip champagne. Besides, I must be getting home. I'm expecting a call from my father in Holland and I wouldn't want to miss it."

"Oh, your father is Dutch?"

Julia shook her head. "No, he's an Aussie. He works in Holland with the Australian Embassy – has for a number of years now."

"Then we must make sure you don't miss your call. Let me signal my car." He pulled out his small cell phone and keyed in several digits. "It will be around front by the time we go down." He dropped the phone back into his pocket.

When the car came to a halt in front of her apartment block, Seth climbed out and escorted her to the door.

She smiled up into his tawny eyes. "Thank you, so much, for giving me the opportunity to bid farewell to Tuthmosis. I know it must seem silly, but ever since I first saw that statue, I've felt almost haunted by it. Hopefully, I'll be able to begin concentrating on my landscapes again." She held out her hand. "Goodbye, Seth."

He took her hand, but instead of shaking it, he gently drew her closer until their bodies almost met. Then slowly, he lowered his head until his lips were a hair's breadth from hers. "Not goodbye," he murmured, "Never goodbye, Julia."

He didn't give her a chance to respond to his words; his lips descended and all other thought fled Julia's mind. Desire spread through her in a delicious warmth and for the space of one heartbeat, she remembered the dream. But as fast as it came, it flitted away again; the power and heat from Seth's mouth claimed all her attention. A damp heat surged through her as she leaned closer and opened to him. Her arms slid upward until her fingers gripped his shoulders; she needed something solid to hold on to. His tongue quested, filling her, robbing her of breath and thought, transporting her beyond place, beyond time.

And for long seconds, as he kissed her, she felt as if she'd finally come home.

The insistent buzz of his cell phone forced them apart. He placed the phone to his ear and listened, his gaze never once leaving her face.

"I'll be there in ten." He flipped the device shut and gave a slight grimace. "I must get back to the office. May I call you this evening?"

Still stunned, all she could do was nod.

He took her hand and brushed her knuckles with his lips, all the time watching her face with the promise of fire sparking deep in his eyes. Suddenly she found it difficult to swallow.

"Tonight," he murmured before retracing his steps and climbing into the car.

"Dear, Lord," she muttered to herself as the vibrant sensations continued to flow through her. "What have I begun?"

Four

Inscription, Tomb 100, Rekh-mi-re, Vizier, Tuthmosis III, Sheikh Abd el-Qurna, Theban Necropolis:

Behold! I bade all My Lord's army search the entire two lands for she who holds My Lord's heart Behold! The rebel princes met their end as all traitors do

Eyes still closed, Julia reached across to grab the handset from the telephone to stop its infernal ringing! As she held it to her ear, she groaned. In her mind's eye she could see a fading snapshot of her stalker as her nightmare disintegrated. Her heart thumped hard as it slowed.

"How's my Jules?" Her father's voice came through clearly from across the other side of the Atlantic.

"What time is it, Dad?" she asked, breathing deeply and squeezed her eyes shut in an attempt to erase the disturbing image that haunted her.

"Eleven p.m. here, sweetheart – that should make it around five there, if I'm not mistaken. You sound very groggy – were you sleeping or have you had a few too many?"

"Actually, Dad, I have to plead guilty on all counts. I drank champagne with lunch and must have dozed off while waiting for your call. How are you?"

"You never could handle alcohol during the day. To answer your question, I'm fine. And so is your mother. We've just been informed we can take some leave in the next couple of months."

She sat up straight, her attention caught. "Are you coming to the States?"

"That is one option, of course, but there's another." His voice sounded hesitant and Julia waited for the shoe to drop.

"An acquaintance has offered us a berth on one of those cruise boats which travel down the Nile. We were thinking of taking it. There is room for up to four in the cabin, so your mother suggested you might like to fly over and join us."

Her heart began to pound. *Egypt*? It seemed almost a kind of synchronicity – only a few months ago she'd never even thought about the place, but since seeing the exhibit, her whole life seemed centered around it. And one of the country's former rulers in particular. What she wouldn't give to explore Tuthmosis's homeland, go to Thebes – perhaps tread the same paths he'd walked all those thousands of years ago.

"You're asking me to come to Egypt? For a cruise down the Nile?"

"Yes. Of course, we'll spring for your air ticket – you being a struggling artist and all. So I guess the question is: are you interested? I know there are probably a lot of other places in the world where you'd rather vacation, but your mother is anxious to spend some time with you."

Her face broke into a broad grin as she twirled the phone cord around her finger. "What makes you think I wouldn't like Egypt, Dad?"

"Oh, I don't know–" Julia could hear the smile in his voice. "–I do recall, when you were about fifteen, you ranting and raving about old places being musty and unexciting. You used to ask why we couldn't go to New York where everything was modern and you could ... what was the term you used? ... 'shop until you drop'?"

A giggle erupted from Julia. "Da-a-ad. I was just a kid. How was I to know anything about culture at that age? And you know I hate shopping. I'd love to come – it's just a matter of whether I can time it with the deadlines I have to meet."

"Well, how about you look into it and let us know when would best suit you. We're reasonably flexible – we have a window of about a month to take the cruise. Why don't you call us in a couple of days and we'll see if we can cement the plans. Is that enough time?"

"Yeah, sure. And by the way, I can pay for my own ticket ... one of the reasons I wanted to talk to you was to tell you I've sold several paintings. One ... wait for it ... for one hundred thousand dollars."

A strange choking noise came down the line.

"Dad? Are you okay? You're not having a heart attack are you? –Dad?"

An instant later he came back on line with a breathless voice. "Sorry sweetheart, I dropped the phone. I thought you said you'd sold a painting for a hundred thousand dollars."

"I did."

There was a long pause, and Julia knew her father was having trouble digesting her revelation. But he surprised her by saying, "In that case maybe you can send your mother and me on a round-the-world trip – Egypt be hanged!"

Julia laughed. "Not on your life. I intend to use the money wisely."

"And spending the money on your doting parents isn't wise?"

"Seriously, Dad. I'd love to. But this is the opportunity I've been waiting for. I can now give up all the weddings and christenings and concentrate on what I love most – apart from you, of course.

"Besides, I might find some wonderful inspiration while cruising down the Nile."

"I'm glad, sweetheart. And very proud, just as your mother will be when I tell her. So, you'll call me in a couple of days so we can get plans for this trip in motion?"

"Definitely, Dad. Give Mum my love, okay?"

"I will. Bye."

"Bye, Dad."

As she placed the phone back in its cradle, her head began to spin. Egypt. She was going to Egypt! A myriad of possibilities began to form in her mind as she headed for the shower, her chest bubbling with excitement.

All vestiges of her unsettling dream had long since escaped her memory – like most dreams, if she didn't concentrate on it as soon as she woke up, it was lost altogether. But it didn't matter. She had plans to make.

*

"I thought you were going to call, not turn up on my doorstep," Julia said as she swung the door open to find Seth standing there dressed in black tie as if ready to attend a formal function. Or perhaps he'd already been – it was, after all, quite late.

"That was my intention when we parted earlier." He surveyed her sleepwear – satin 'Pink Panther' pajamas – with a bemused expression as he stepped inside. "I see that I've caught you at a bad time. I merely wanted to apologize for not calling when I'd promised. Several foreign dignitaries with whom our bank has been trying to forge a relationship, chose this afternoon to begin discussions. Unfortunately, the one opportunity I got to call you – your line was busy."

"That's okay, I was probably still talking to Dad," she replied. "You didn't stand me up – it's not as though we had a date or anything."

"No? I thought it was – even if only a phone call."

After closing the door, she turned and lifted an eyebrow. "Oh?"

"My father raised me to honor my promises, no matter how insignificant they might seem to another."

The corner of her lips lifted. "Then I should thank you for your consideration. Would you like a coffee, or a glass of wine?"

"Coffee'd be good – I need it. It's been a long night and these men I'm dealing with are ruthless businessmen. They care nothing for people or circumstances, only the bottom line, so I couldn't let down my guard for a minute."

He followed her into the kitchen and leaned against the doorframe as she set about making their coffee. He watched as she unclipped the jar which she'd retrieved from the freezer and placed two large spoonfuls into the percolator.

"You do like it strong, don't you?" she said as she returned the canister to a shelf in the freezer. "I've been told I'm nuts, but I love a rich cup late at night."

"Strong is fine."

Studying her actions, he mused over her guileless grace. None of her movements were deliberately seductive, yet she seduced him with ease. He wondered how long he was going to be able to keep his distance. He'd wanted her from the minute he'd laid eyes on her. Something in her called to him. From that very first instant, he'd felt as if his soul had met its twin and with each passing moment that belief strengthened.

Even his cousin Beth knew. She'd seen it in his eyes as he walked through the door after dropping Julia home from their lunch at the museum.

"You've found her, haven't you," Beth had said.

He didn't reply, because he'd thought so before only to be disappointed. Yet, this time it was stronger. The call, the ache ... the need ... was far more intense. So much so, he felt almost consumed by it.

Thus, he'd wound up standing on her doorstep at nearly ten.

When he couldn't get her on the phone, he decided to send a note and flowers in the morning to apologize. But as he drove home, the car seemed to detour on its own, and he hadn't noticed where he headed until he found himself only a street away. He'd sat downstairs in his car and stared up at her apartment for a full ten minutes, watching her shadow move about behind the blinds in the living room before he surrendered to the urge and made his way up to her floor. Now he was glad he did. Her presence seemed to cure a restlessness in him.

"Black or cream?"

"If you have cream, I won't say no."

She pulled a face and shivered. "Can't stand the stuff – I just keep it for unannounced 'drop ins'," she glanced up, her greenish eyes twinkling, "like you."

"Then all us 'drop ins' thank you," he said gallantly, returning her grin.

"Sugar?"

He shook his head.

"Me neither," she commented, leading him back into the living room to sit at the small table by her front window. "So, was your meeting successful?"

With a sigh he sat back and swirled the liquid in his cup. "In a manner of speaking, though I'm not sure I like doing business with these people – negotiations will be slow and delicate, requiring more concentration than I'd anticipated. Time will tell."

"But what of your phone call – are your parents well?" he asked.

Her eyes lit up. "As a matter of fact, my dad had great news when he called. You know how I said I'd be unlikely to ever see Tuthmosis's relics again?"

He nodded.

"Well, that might not be true, after all. My parents have managed to arrange a cruise down the Nile and have asked me to join them." She obviously wanted to keep a tight rein on her excitement but he could tell it threatened to burst out.

"When?"

"In a few weeks, I expect. I have to work out the best time to get away then call Dad back on Wednesday. Hopefully our plans can coincide for some time late in October. I might even travel about a bit afterward."

Seth worked hard to prevent himself from frowning. Although he dearly wanted her to see his family's homeland – he also wanted to be the one to show it to her. Not her parents or some faceless riverboat captain. And he didn't think he'd be able to get away so soon to accompany her. Still, he'd orchestrated more difficult arrangements in the past.

"I have family in various places. If you give me the dates, I can organize to have them show you the real Egypt. And my bank owns several top class hotels – there are always suites freely available for employee use."

"But I'm not an employee."

"Perhaps not, but we could pretend you're my fiancée or something. They'll never know the difference."

"But—"

"Forget about 'buts.'" He took her hand in his and smoothed the skin on the back with his thumb. Ripples of sensation danced along his arm. She quickly drew her hand away but the rising color in her cheeks told him she'd felt it too.

"You know what they say about 'gift horses,'" he cautioned. "One of my cousins, I think, works for the tourist bureau coordinating Valley of the Kings and Abu Simbel excursions. Perhaps you'd like to go on one of those?"

"Oh, Seth, do you think I can? – that'd be fabulous," she exclaimed with almost child-like wonder. "To see those giant statues ... it's simply beyond my imagination. And, of course, I'd have to go to Giza and see the pyramids. No one can go to Egypt and not visit them."

"Well," he cleared his throat and tried to calm his own feelings, "just let me know when you're flying over, and the cruise dates, and I'll make inquiries. It is unfortunate I'll be unable to escort you myself – it would be a joy to see my ancestors' homeland through your eyes."

She looked up and met Seth's gaze. "Yeah, it'd be nice to have someone I know, who loves the country, show me the sights."

"Why, Ms Morrow, keep talking like that and I might take it as an invitation," he warned with a broad smile.

She tilted her head. "I thought you were embarking on, how did you put it? – 'delicate negotiations' that you couldn't leave?"

"You're quite right. So I am." He stood and circled the table. "I expect I should let you go to bed. You must be tired."

She shook her head. "Not at all."

"Another invitation, perhaps?" he murmured, moving a step closer. He knew she meant nothing of the sort. She was simply being candid, but he couldn't resist teasing her. And the look of alarm she wore was priceless.

Julia straightened and backed up a pace. "If you must know, I took a bit of a nap this afternoon – a strange man plied me with expensive champagne, which made me very sleepy.

"I was just preparing to paint when you arrived, wasn't I, Bird?" She directed her question to the silent parrot that'd been sleeping on his perch across the room the entire time since Seth's arrival. Bird turned his head at the mention of his name, blinked once, before burying his head under one wing.

"Traitor," she murmured.

With a laugh Seth eased a step closer to her. "I was only teasing, Julia. I promise not to seduce you unless, of course, you ask to be seduced." He took her hand and drew it to his lips, just as he'd done earlier.

Suddenly, she found herself staring into the very depths of his eyes. His pupils grew as he met her gaze and the amber irises darkened until they seemed the color of warm chocolate. She felt herself inching toward them as if lost, and those eyes would somehow guide her home.

Seth closed the space between their mouths and claimed her essence in the very same second as he claimed her lips. It began as a soft kiss, full of giving, his lips cherished hers as they explored. Then as the heat within her started to intensify the kiss became stronger, more demanding. Yet she was eager to give. The sensations he evoked were so rich and new, she cared for nothing beyond the moment. Soft, moist, warmth became strength, dampness and fire. All conscious thought seeped away as she pressed herself against his hard chest. Her body had a will of its own and it was literally drowning in a myriad of unknown feelings. No man had caused such a reaction in her and it seemed beyond her control to stop it.

The power of her reaction became almost frightening. She needed a foothold, an anchor. Her hands crept up his arms until they held the thick tail tied at his nape. How she wished she could release it and feel his shiny black hair sliding through her fingers. An image from her dreams flashed across her mind ... of Seth above her, his long hair falling like a curtain around her face as he made love to her. It was as if, for an instant, they had blended into one being.

She quivered and the image disappeared as quickly as it came.

Ever so slowly, he began to withdraw. His kiss gentled, again transforming, until his touch became as delicate as a gossamer wing, before he abandoned her altogether.

"Ohhh." The breathy sound escaped before she had the chance to stop it. She covered her mouth with her hand, though she didn't know whether she did so because her lips felt bruised or she wanted to hold onto the sensation that remained there.

Not in her wildest dreams could she have imagined such an intensity of emotion.

Seth spun away and shuddered noticeably. When he turned back his face appeared torn by some unnamed emotion, then he broke into a rueful smile. "Yes ... *'Ohhh'* would be an apt description."

Julia didn't know what to say. Maybe she should have seen it coming, but nothing could have prepared her for that. She simply didn't believe a kiss could make her whole being react.

She looked away – his expression asked too much.

"Well ... ," he murmured after a long moment. "What do we do now?"

"Do? Why do we have to do anything?" Dear Lord, she needed to retreat – needed to think.

"Mmmm – do," he said thoughtfully. "You know, of course, we can't just walk away from this."

"No?" Her eyes widened as he took her shoulders in a firm grip.

"No. Don't expect me to. We can take things slowly if that's what you need – but I can't walk away. Not now." Even as he said the words, he knew he lied. They had very little time. And now he knew for certain that she was the one, time was a luxury they couldn't afford to waste. Both their lives could very well depend on it.

"But–"

He placed a forefinger over her lips to prevent her voicing whatever argument she'd begun to formulate, then rested his forehead against hers for a moment. "I'll go now," he murmured. "But only to give you some space to grow accustomed to the idea of us."

Her eyelids drifted closed as she sighed. "But there is no *us* – I'm not sure I'm ready for an *us*."

His fingertips traced up her jaw and then buried themselves in her hair, holding her still so she couldn't evade his potent gaze. "Look at me, Julia."

Her eyelids fluttered and rose. Her irises darkened as their eyes met and held.

"A wise man once said there is no such thing as an accident – everything occurs as it should, when it should. Some call it fate. I call it destiny. And now I'm sure. You're my destiny, as I am yours." Brushing a chaste kiss on her brow he released her completely. "I knew it the instant I saw you.

"I'll ring you tomorrow so we can get together and talk more," he promised.

Before she could utter a single word, he'd grabbed his car keys and disappeared out her front door.

As if in a trance, she walked to the door and slid the bolt home. Her hands were shaking and her heart drummed a violent beat it never had before. In a matter of days her world had turned upside down.

Picking up her coffee, she moved to the window to stare out through the narrow gap in the blinds at the streetlights below. Another surge of adrenalin flooded her belly as she watched him walk to his car.

Almost absently, she noted that someone sat on the bench at the bus stop across the street, which was odd, since the last bus went by some time ago.

Five

A rabid smile stretched across his face as he turned to embrace the woman standing alongside him. "That should do it," he said running his fingertips down her naked back until he found the cleft of her bottom.

She wriggled away, her liquid gaze playful and full of promises. "Yes – the little rabbit should run a mile when she hears it. I wish I could be there to see it."

"She's nothing so it makes no difference – simply a means to an end."

Malice made his companion's eyes glisten like shards of dark glass.

To his mind, she made the perfect partner for this endeavor; she seemed to have no heart at all. She was sexy and without conscience – meeting her had been a godsend. Though if their comrade could be believed, everything about their coming together had been preordained. He didn't know about that, and nor did he care, so long as he got what he wanted.

"Are you sure no one will trace the call?" she asked.

"Of course – we weren't be on the line long enough. Anyway, the number is restricted – they'd have to get a warrant to find out and by that time we'll be long gone."

"As long as you're sure."

He kissed her, hard and fast. "You worry too much."

*

The members of the board filed into the expansive boardroom and sat in their usual places around the enormous table. Seth, with his secretary by his side, was the last to take his chair.

Although Seth held the position of CEO, Martin Willis had been Chairman of the Board since the bank first opened its doors in Boston. Martin, with a solid background in international banking, kept a very conservative outlook and Seth often found himself at odds with the man's 'go slow' attitude. Seth believed the only way the bank could gain a greater foothold in the community was to be more progressive and proactive, especially in their international brokering and share trading activities on behalf of the bank's bigger shareholders. Martin, however, always played it safe and tended to veto or water down many of the operational suggestions Seth tabled.

"Good afternoon, gentlemen," Martin said in his usual somber voice.

As they sat through the recitation of minutes of the previous meeting, Seth's mind kept straying to Julia and her denial of their growing relationship. As far as he was concerned, she could deny all she liked, because he knew differently. Her eyes said differently. He just wondered if he might be able to swing a lightning trip back to Egypt whilst she vacationed there with her parents. They'd have to meet him sooner or later, and to his mind, the sooner the better – especially if that introduction could take place at his ancestral home. Besides, he hadn't lied – he'd give just about anything to act as her guide.

"Seth?"

With a quick shake of his head, he turned toward his secretary.

"Yes, Carolynne?"

"Would you like the paperwork you prepared on overnight and short-term money market investment tabled now?"

He nodded, hoping he hadn't missed too much, but at the same time confident that Carolynne had recorded every word said and would have transcribed within an hour of the meeting's close.

Carolynne stood and passed a red folder and attached thumb drive to each board member in turn, then handed the floor over to Seth. He took up the remote and the screen behind him came to life.

"Gentlemen, ladies, I believe the short term international monetary markets will allow us to make solid investment profits for our large shareholders, without having to trim services to our smaller stakeholders – and still stimulate overall profit.

"I've had a series of simulations done, if you'll look at graphs four and five," he clicked to the desired page, "which demonstrate the viability of placing overnight investments in well chosen foreign currencies. As you can see, several of the dummy investments made small losses, but overall the profit ran at more than twenty-three percent over a 12 month period."

Seth went on to explain his plan in greater detail, careful to give a full report on both the positive and negative aspects of the plan.

"I suggest that we approach some of our larger shareholders and clients, and gauge their reaction to such a plan," Martin interjected, scratching his balding head, "after all, it's their money we're talking about."

"Certainly," Seth agreed. "Meanwhile, we should continue the simulations – that way we have a longer term view of viability."

"Yup, those profits could have been beginner's luck," remarked Edward Milliou, whose resources stemmed from the breeding of fine thoroughbred racehorses.

Seth smiled. "Perhaps, but I believe if we do our homework on this, we can generate a great deal of profit for our shareholders."

"How about we all study the paperwork and review the proposal at our monthly meeting on the first."

Each man, in turn, nodded his agreement.

"So, if there's nothing further, we can close the meeting," Martin said and began to pack the stack of papers on the table before him.

When no one objected, Carolynne said, "Meeting closed at 1:10 p.m. Minutes will be available at four – I'll email a copy to everyone then."

*

Across the table, Irene prattled on about some new artist she'd discovered. Julia didn't hear a word of the one-sided conversation and didn't particularly care. She'd spent a dreamless – no make that sleepless

– night, tossing and turning. She'd been besieged by images of Seth looming over her, kissing her, and vowing to keep her with him forever. But at some point he became the pharaoh of her dreams, someone her imagination conjured from the photograph.

Certainly not the Seth she'd kissed last night.

And in a way that lay at the heart of the problem causing her sleeplessness. She didn't honestly know whether she felt attracted to the real-life Seth, or the phantom pharaoh who'd taken on Seth's face in her dreaming mind. It felt like she was betraying one of them, but she just didn't know which.

What if her feelings for the man turned out to be a lie because she'd become obsessed by a statue made of stone?

And worse, she'd begun planning to take a trip to Egypt, which would only feed that obsession.

God – I need a psychiatrist.

"Yeow!" she complained when Irene poked her arm. "Why'd you do that?"

Lowering her sunglasses so Julia could take in the full measure of her disgusted glare, Irene snorted, "You haven't heard a single word I've said. If I wanted to be ignored, I'd have married long ago."

With a sigh, Julia tried to smile and focus. "Sorry, Irene. I didn't sleep last night and now I can barely string together a coherent train of thought. What were you saying?"

"I *said* – that you've managed to accumulate quite a bank from the exhibition. Gerry did hand over that first check, didn't he?"

Julia nodded.

Irene passed a similar envelope across the table. "Here's most of the rest. One or two clients are yet to settle, but almost all have. You might just make me rich, yet."

Quirking a brow, Julia opened the envelope and gasped. The check read one hundred and thirty seven thousand dollars, and a few odd cents. "But what about your commission?"

"Already deducted."

"But how–?"

"Several buyers tried to outbid each other when they learned how much your pharaoh portrait fetched."

"But how could any of the other buyers possibly know the price?"

Irene assumed an expression of utter innocence, before breaking into a broad grin. "I told them, of course. After all, their purchases are all the more valuable once people become aware you sold a six digit piece."

"Six digit?" As far as she could recall, none of the pharaoh's fingers were visible in the portrait.

"The hundred thou' price tag ... you weren't kidding when you said you couldn't think straight." With a mother hen sense of purpose, Irene removed Julia's untouched glass of wine and motioned to the waiter.

"Two strong mochas – to have straight away, your largest cups, if you please," she informed the young woman. Turning back to Julia she continued, "We can't have you falling asleep in your lunch."

Their pasta salads arrived along with the coffee and once she'd digested a little of each, Julia began to feel a tad more human.

"So, has he called?" Irene asked in between bites of grilled octopus.

Julia feigned ignorance. "Has who called?"

It always amazed Julia how Irene could make every single muscle in her face frown when she wanted to – and she did so now.

"You know perfectly well, who. Seth Almose, of course. Gerry told me you two were having an intimate meal at the museum yesterday."

"If you knew that, why did you ask about the check?" Julia challenged as she stabbed at an unsuspecting shrimp, only to have it slide right off the plate.

With a careless lift of her shoulder, Irene shrugged.

"And why would you expect him to call so soon?"

Again Irene shrugged. "I guess I hoped you'd tell me all about it without me having to prise every tidbit of information as if I were extracting teeth."

Tossing her fork aside, Julia wiped her mouth with her napkin and slumped back in her chair.

Irene smirked at Julia's discomfort.

"It was obvious he was very taken with you at the showing. So – what gives? Tell Auntie Irene all about it," she cajoled, gracefully popping an olive into her mouth.

Eyes narrowed, Julia considered her options, but knew it'd be useless to avoid the subject – Irene could be persistent when she set her mind to it. Ruthlessly so.

"Oh, what the heck, you'll find out soon enough. He came over last night and, from what he said, I think he wants to pursue a relationship. I've told him I'll think about it."

"Did you sleep with him?"

Julia's eyes widened with affront. "No! How can you ask me that? I've never slept with a man at the first meeting. What do you think I am?" she demanded.

Leaning across the table to pat Julia's hand, Irene sought to mollify her young friend. "Relax. It wasn't the first meeting – it was your third if my math is correct. Besides, I thought we decided all you really needed was a good lay."

Julia's cheeks paled as she glanced around. "Tell the whole restaurant, Irene!" She leaned forward and whispered urgently, "And you were the one who decided I needed to get laid, not me. I'm quite happy the way things are and I'm certainly not going to launch into a full-blown love affair simply because you think I should."

Crossing her arms, Julia signaled that there'd be no further discussion.

"Fine," Irene agreed. "But, before you discard the possibility, just take a moment and count up all the pluses. He's gorgeous," she held up her index finger, "he has to have a fairly healthy bank balance, after all he's president of some bank or another," she held up her middle finger, "he's not married, I checked–"

Julia reached over, gripped Irene's fingers and scrunched them. "You did what?"

"Oh don't get your panties twisted – I simply made a few discreet inquiries to find out if he was heart-breaker material. For your protection. My sources say he hasn't had a serious relationship in a while. The woman with him at the opening, Hannah el-somethingorother, was his girlfriend at one time, and there was a flight attendant, Celine, umm, Stephens? Steele?" she scratched her temple thoughtfully, "can't remember exactly ... but apparently things didn't work out and he called it off a couple of years ago.

"Born in Egypt with an English mother, Seth's lived in the U.S. since he was four years old. His father worked as an investment broker before he retired back to Egypt some eight years ago. Seth attended the University of California, has an honors degree in Finance and Accounting, and a masters in Ancient History – specifically, you guessed it – Egypt. He came to Boston two years ago, last April, to take over the reins at the bank."

"Irene ... how could you possibly learn all that so quickly? And – just so you know, I don't think it's very ethical of you to go digging around in people's private affairs."

Irene dismissed her protests with a wave. "Listen, my dear, someone has to look out for your welfare. Your parents are in Europe. Your brother is AWOL somewhere in the Australian outback. So it's up to me to make sure you don't get into trouble or have your heart broken. She nodded once as if to say 'enough said'.

"In case you hadn't noticed, Irene, I'm a big girl now. At twenty-three I can take care of my own love life, thanks."

"Oh, pooh. Don't be such a worrier – I'm just doing what any big sister would do. And since I have no little sister, and you have no big sister, I think I can assume the role without treading on anyone's toes. Besides, most of the info is in the public domain. I'd have thought you'd have googled him."

Julia felt too weary to argue anymore. She supposed that knowing a little of Seth's background didn't really hurt. And she guessed he'd done a bit of sleuthing about her, too, since he'd already known her address before she offered it. She also knew that Irene meant well, even if, at times she came across somewhat heavy-handed.

"Are we finished with lunch?" Julia asked, suddenly desperate for a few hours sleep.

"Yes, I'm all done." Irene tucked her neatly folded her napkin beside her plate and motioned to the waiter to bring the bill. "I'll let you buy, seeing as you're now a rich woman."

Julia grinned. "Hardly rich. But certainly better off than a month ago," she said, waving the check-filled envelope in the air. "I'll have to go home via the bank."

"Any bank in particular?" Irene raised a perfectly arched brow.

"Sorry, Irene, I'm not playing that game. You can drop me at the mall and I'll go to my usual branch. Then, I'm going to go home, take a long bath, and crash until sometime next week. So don't bother calling – the phone will be off the hook."

"To everyone? Or just me?" Irene asked with a suggestive grin.

"Forget whatever you're thinking – I'll be incommunicado to *everyone*."

A shadow fell across the table as Julia reached down to retrieve her purse. For long seconds she didn't recognize the man's face as the sun shone from directly behind him. But as she stood, his identity became all too obvious.

"Hello, boss," Gerry greeted. "Hi, Julia."

Julia nodded a mute hello.

"What brings you here, Gerry?" Irene asked, her expression perplexed. "I thought you were meeting with Sebastian's lawyer to sign that contract at two."

Gerry brandished the papers as if he held a great prize.

"All done. I was just on my way back to the gallery when I saw you two sitting here, so I decided I'd join you for a quick cup of coffee to celebrate Julia's success. My treat." He leaned in close and invaded Julia's space. The smile he bestowed lacked either warmth or humor.

That's it! Julia realized. The thing that always made her feel so wary was the way Gerry always presumed to take over. Instead of exuding an image of assured confidence, his forward manner came across as pushy and manipulative.

And to add weight to her inner argument, he gripped her arm firmly. "So sit, both of you – I'll just go inside and order. Would either of you ladies care for cake, or a liqueur with your coffee?"

An overwhelming desire to escape took hold of Julia and for once she didn't fight it. "I'm sorry Gerry, but I really can't stay – I have business to attend to at the bank before it closes. You understand, don't you?"

The harsh expression that momentarily crossed his face made her want to shrink backward. And for a split second, he reminded her of someone else, though the memory lay at the very edge of her mind and she couldn't quite bring it into focus. Somehow she knew that she ought to avoid being alone with this man.

Just the idea sent a chill coursing down her spine.

"Another time, perhaps," he said in a smooth tone that promised he would indeed follow up.

"Yes," she replied, as she laid two fifties on the waiter's tray. "Maybe next week."

With a kiss for Irene and a distant smile for Gerry, she made for the corner. By the time she'd moved beyond sight of the restaurant she felt breathless and drained.

Forget the bank, she thought. *I'll go tomorrow.* Instead, she hailed a cab and went straight home.

*

When she arrived home, Julia noticed the message light flashing on her answering machine. She'd been expecting several calls from clients, one of whom had offered a staggering commission if she'd paint a portrait of his favorite Roman emperor, Trajan. She didn't know if her talent extended to such a feat, but the sum quoted couldn't be dismissed.

She flicked the play button and set about filling the kettle as she listened. The first message, obviously recorded earlier in the day was Irene reminding her of their lunch date. The second: just a series of clicks – no doubt the caller hated answer machines as much as she did – and had simply hung up.

The third message made her pause, her hand stopping mid-air as she reached for a mug.

It started with what sounded like a growl and then, "You think you have him, bitch? ..."

After a long moment of silence, "... well, I've got news for you," the voice ground out in low, hostile tones.

Julia blinked several times wondering what on earth the voice on the tape was talking about? The voice sounded so deep and slurry, she couldn't even tell the caller's gender.

Just as she reached out a shaky finger to shut the device off, the voice spoke again. She snatched her hand back as if a snake had coiled itself around the machine, ready to strike.

"Bitch, I'm warning you. Don't see him again. Don't touch him. Don't any...thing ... with him, or you'll learn the hard way – and that pretty little face of yours won't be so pretty anymore. Got it, bitch? He doesn't belong to you. Keep your paws off!"

The machine stopped with a sudden snap. Julia jumped back, her heart racing.

Her first conscious thought was to call Seth and seek his comfort. How it had happened in such a short space of time, she didn't know, but she felt safe with him. Intuitively, she knew he'd protect her.

But if the voice on the machine wasn't some hoax, that's exactly what she couldn't do. The warning left no room for uncertainty – stay away from Seth, or else.

She shook her head, trying to dismiss the message as someone's idea of a practical joke, yet deep down, she knew otherwise. Whoever had made that call sounded deadly serious.

After thoroughly checking the locks on all her windows and doors, she found it very difficult to sleep, despite her intense fatigue. She spent much of the night fading in and out of nightmares, pursued by a faceless shadow that stood menacingly between her and the statue of Tuthmosis.

*

The figures that lit up his computer screen were nothing short of dazzling. He'd done it – and it was so damned easy! More money than he'd dreamed, all in a matter of minutes. Using borrowed client funds he'd made a killing on the overnight money market. He knew he'd been very lucky, but at the same time it was a calculated kind of luck. He'd watched the markets for weeks and made his choices prudently using the simulations as a model.

Now all he needed to do was divert the funds into the accounts he'd set up.

He'd watched and waited until he knew all the night shift personnel had stopped for their half-hour meal break before using the root-privilege password to alter the server's internal clock – thus creating the illusion this transaction occurred hours before the client withdrawals had taken place, then he initiated the first transfer.

The Jersey and Cayman Islands accounts had been opened months ago, ready for his assault. His eyes gleamed as the window popped up saying, 'transfer complete' on the first transaction – his own secret account in Jersey, which he'd camouflaged behind layers of shelf companies and dummy corporations based in various places around the world.

He quickly returned the computer's clock to the correct time, logged out, then logged in under an alternate password. His password. For the next several hours while he waited for the night shift to finish, he processed a whole range of legitimate transactions to separate the other transfers from the first one in terms of time. There'd be no readily visible connection on the printed reports.

Next he pulled up the relevant shareholder and client files and, one by one, returned the borrowed funds, noting on each file that the withdrawals were errors. He deliberately transposed the date field and the amount field on each transaction to make the mistakes appear legitimate, then, simply reversed the transactions. Easy. Anyone checking would assume the data input operator had made a series of harmless blunders that were corrected as soon as the operator realized.

At least, at first glance they would – but if they chose to scrutinize a little more closely, they'd see the pattern. When the time ripened, he'd show the right person what he'd *stumbled* upon.

Now, to the second transaction. He didn't bother to suppress the smirk on his face as the transfer went through.

"You'll find out the hard way, you bastard." His words were directed at the man whose name appeared on the second level of the Cayman Islands account. He'd made it look like whoever owned the account had attempted to conceal his identity – but not well enough that it wouldn't be traced with a bit of digging on the authorities' part.

He aimed to repeat the process over the next few nights, careful to only place the profits in the second account from tonight onward. That way, the repeated pattern would stick out – and the supposed culprit, his target, would eventually be investigated. Of course, by then, he intended to be long gone. His only regret was that he wouldn't be on hand to see his adversary's face when he realizes he has been set up.

I might just hang around, anyway, he thought to himself, *it'd be too good to miss.*

Six

It felt as if she hadn't slept at all. Julia's brain seemed to be filled with cotton wool, and her thinking was all fuzzy and vague. The night, like most since she'd met Seth, had been plagued by dreams peopled with faces she didn't quite recognize from a time that had become all too familiar. More and more she found herself drifting into the ancient world of her pharaoh, though the events she remembered were so disjointed she hardly understood any of it.

The only thing that did stand out was an increasing sense of danger. Someone's life was under threat. Whose, why, or even when, she didn't begin to comprehend. But she had the distinct impression she ought to do something to help.

"Ha!" she exclaimed as she flopped down against her pillow and closed her eyes. What a ridiculous thought – help people who've been dead for thousands of years. "That's it, it's finally happened, Jules. You're quite insane."

Bird flew into the room, circled once and came to land on her stomach, squawking loudly as he did every morning at that time.

"No droppings on the bed, Bird," she moaned as she threw her forearm across her eyes. "I really should close the door, shouldn't I?"

It was a ritual they'd repeated each day for over a year. Every morning Bird would wake her with the sun, hop around on the bed and make a grand pretence of inspecting the frilly coverlet, for what she couldn't imagine, then he'd shuffle his way up her stomach to her chest and sit watching her face until she deemed to acknowledge him and say, "Okay, Bird, time for breakfast."

As soon as he heard that last word, off he'd fly, back to his perch, and sit dancing and bobbing until Julia brought fresh seed and water. It had become one of those games people play with their pets that gave the world order and predictability.

"Ohhh!" she gripped her forehead once she sat upright. If she didn't know better, she'd have sworn she was heading for an alcohol-induced migraine.

Padding to the kitchen, she turned on the kettle and set about changing Bird's food and water. Once the seed was placed before him, Bird ignored Julia completely to concentrate on his meal.

A strong cup of chamomile tea and two aspirins later, Julia showered and dressed and prepared for a day in the darkroom. If she intended to meet her parents for the trip down the Nile, she needed to get all her photographic commitments behind her.

"Of course," she said out loud as her mind played over the possibility that'd hovered in the back of her mind the past day or so.

Now I've got some money, I could hire an assistant for a week, maybe two.

Once she'd prepared the chemicals, she emerged from the darkroom and went to the phone. Irene knew a number of photographers; surely one of them had an assistant she could borrow for a short while.

"Hey, Irene," she said when Irene's melodic voice came down the line. "It's Julia."

"Hello. What can I do for my best client so early in the morning? How are things going with that handsome banker of yours?"

Julia paused and frowned fiercely. "If you mean Seth, A: he's not *my* banker, and B: I haven't seen him."

"Oh? I thought you were going to meet him after our lunch the other day," Irene said suggestively.

Tensing slightly, Julia wished she could just tell Irene to back off and stop trying to interfere with her love life, non-existent as it was. But she knew she couldn't. Irene had been there for her when she really needed a friend. First she'd helped Julia when she arrived alone and afraid after fleeing Australia. She'd secured her a position with a photographic company until Julia found her feet and could build a client base. Then she'd shown confidence in Julia's talent by supporting her painting. Of all the people in the world, Irene had the right to meddle, even if it made Julia a little crazy.

"There are many reasons to go to the bank, Irene. Besides, I told you I was going to my local branch. I had several checks to deposit … remember?'

"Mmmm, I thought you lied so I'd mind my own business." Irene said in a voice that sounded resentful but Julia knew it was all an act.

"I'd never lie to you Irene – that is asking for trouble!'

"You bet it is," Irene laughed, "and don't ever forget it. So why the early call?"

Julia sat back and rubbed her forehead. The headache had improved, but only marginally. "I'm thinking of hiring a good photographic assistant for a week or two, just until I can finish up all the backlog. After the current orders are finished, I'll give it away for a while, perhaps even sell the business. Is there anyone you could recommend?"

There was a long silence at the other end of the line, then Irene said, "Let me ask a few of the people I know and I'll call you back. Is that all right?"

"Sure. I'll be here all day." She couldn't imagine going anywhere while her head pounded like it did.

Probably caffeine withdrawal, she thought, realizing she hadn't yet had her morning coffee. Once she hung up the phone, she made herself an espresso.

Several hours later, an array of enlargements hung from the row of tiny pegs strung across the darkroom. A number of the group shots looked promising in the proofs, but she wouldn't be certain about the enlargements until she looked at them in ordinary daylight. Then she'd know if she had to mask or burn in any detail. These were the black and white set requested by the bride. The digital color files had gone to a specialist lab in town, and she'd select those enlargements later in the week.

The phone rang just as she pulled aside the black curtain screen that she used to cover the door when she worked in the darkroom.

"It's only me," Irene said when Julia picked up the receiver. "Gerry's on his way over ... he has a proposition for you."

"Gerry?" *A proposition?* The hair at Julia's nape prickled.

"Yes," Irene answered, excitement evident in her voice. "I'll let him tell you."

"But—"

Julia drew the hand piece away from her ear and looked at it as if it was an alien object, then put it to her ear again. All she heard was the electronic wail of a dead line.

Despite the urge to call Irene back to find out what it was all about, Julia placed the handset in its cradle and headed for the bathroom. For some reason, one she couldn't consciously fathom, she felt the need to prepare herself for a meeting with Gerry.

After scrubbing her face clean, she gave her teeth a good brushing then went to the bedroom to change out of her old work clothes and into jeans and a neat, businesslike blouse, which buttoned high at her throat. Finally, she pulled her wheat-colored hair back into a severe ponytail and tied it. Whatever Gerry had in mind, she expected she wasn't going to feel comfortable with it. She just prayed he wasn't going to ask her to employ his friend, Tobias – she'd only met him once or twice but he gave her the creeps.

Recalling Gerry's horror at his one and only meeting with Bird, she positioned the perch alongside the chair where she intended to sit – anything to give her the upper hand.

She'd barely put the perch in place when the doorbell rang twice in quick succession – as if her caller wanted urgent attention. She stifled a groan, stiffened her spine, and went to answer the door. After checking through the peephole to confirm Gerry's identity, she eased the door open.

Dressed in his immaculately tailored suit with his perfectly styled hair, as glossy and black and neat as always, he reminded her more of an unscrupulous car salesman than an art appraiser. He stared at her in a probing kind of way and like an inexperienced schoolgirl, her sense of unease grew. For a split second, she pictured him with a short beard. Why that image came into her mind she didn't know; she couldn't recall him ever wearing a beard and she didn't really have time to think about it now.

"Did Irene call?" he asked without bothering to greet her. His dark eyes seemed to pin her in place before he slipped past and entered the living room.

"Hello, Gerry," she returned pointedly, stressing an equal lack of courtesy. She left the front door open and folded her arms across her chest. "Irene did call, but she didn't say what you wanted."

Turning toward her, he gave her an indulgent smile, the kind that never quite reaches the eyes and always leaves the impression something sinister is about to emerge.

"Won't the parrot fly away?" he asked, glancing down at the strategically placed perch with distaste. She didn't fail to notice he carefully maintained a reasonable distance from Bird's long beak, though.

"Not likely – Bird's very much a homebody. He doesn't like to have me out of his sight."

Gerry's brow creased but he didn't comment. He paced the length of the room then noted the photograph of Tuthmosis.

"Ah, the inspiration," he turned, his forehead creasing. "Strange, I thought you'd had a real model pose for that one."

With a shake of her head, Julia crossed the room, sat alongside Bird and lifted him to her shoulder.

"Stuffaduck ... stuffaduck!" Bird squawked, then immediately set about trying to pluck the band that held her ponytail.

"Stop that," she chided, offering a sunflower seed as a distraction.

"So," Gerry mused after studying the photograph further. "I thought the portrait was commissioned by Almose. That he'd sat for it. I must say, I'm surprised he paid so much for it. I'd assumed his vanity boosted the price."

"Not at all. I met Mr Almose for the first time at the opening and was just as astounded as everyone else when he made the offer. Tuthmosis is reputed to be a distant ancestor of his."

Gerry's head shot around. "Really? That *is* interesting." He moved to the nearby settee and lowered himself onto it, though he remained tensed as if ready to dash away if Bird decided to become in the least friendly. "I imagine it's quite something to be able to trace your family tree back three and a half thousand years."

"Yes. I guess it would be. Now, to the reason you came by?" she raised a brow in question.

He played with his shirt cuffs a moment, a nervous habit she'd noticed on other occasions, then said, "Irene tells me you're in need of an assistant – and that you're also thinking of selling the photographic business."

Julia stilled.

"Well, I'm thinking about it. Do you have a contact that might be interested? I can't pay a great deal in wages, initially the job'd be only two weeks or so," she explained. "And the business is only small at this stage – barely enough to live on, really.

"It's a boutique business in old fashioned photography and restorations ... hardly something someone ambitious would be interested in." She shook her head. "And now, with the advent of such good digital cameras, just about anybody could do their own photographic work."

"Oh, the pay wouldn't matter. For what I have in mind, the business is the important part." He leaned forward, an eager expression spread over his face.

"I couldn't presume to have anyone work for me without wages. Tell me, the person you have in mind, is it someone I know?"

Again he tugged at his cuff.

He stood and stepped closer as if to loom over her though he kept his distance from Bird. "Actually, I've been thinking of breaking out on my own for quite a while."

Him? A cold feeling filled her stomach.

"I don't know whether Irene ever told you," he continued, "but before I went to work for her, I studied photography. I've always intended to have my own studio, with a small gallery attached. This could be the perfect opportunity to make a move in that direction."

Julia looked away. On the surface it appeared the ideal solution. Yet the thought of working with him, day in and day out, for even a week or two, seemed almost nauseating. How could she possibly do it?

"Surely you're not thinking of leaving Irene," she commented in disbelief. "I expect she'll make you gallery manager before too long."

"I am manager, have been for more than a year now – but I don't really have the autonomy I desire. I need to be 'master of my own kingdom', so to speak."

Why did those words sound eerily familiar? A flash from one of her recent dreams raced across her memory and then melted. She drew her brows together.

"What I propose is this: I come and work with you for the next few weeks and brush up on my photographic and darkroom skills. At the same time I'll scout for a new venue for the business – something nearby, to maintain continuity, of course. I'll buy whatever equipment you wish to sell, and the business name, goodwill and such – all at a fair price. And perhaps, at a later date, you might want to work with me sometimes, just to keep a hand in."

He threw her a wry smile and she had to swallow to prevent herself reacting.

"But the business only just returns enough to support me now – how can –?"

"Oh, I have money," he interrupted. "A wealthy forebear left me quite a legacy. So you see, financing is not an issue. I've been looking for just such an opportunity. Your business is the ideal beginning. Once I have that, I'll be a step closer to my ultimate goal."

As she looked at his changing expressions, she had the overwhelming feeling he meant so much more than just her business.

She shook away the sensation. All these strange dreams and lack of proper sleep had sent her imagination into overdrive; nothing Gerry had ever said or done could be construed as wrong or untoward. He might seem overbearing but he'd never actually threatened her in any way. Here he was, offering exactly what she wanted – further, he was willing to work for free. And still she felt reticent. Why?

What was it, precisely, that made her feel in danger whenever he came near her?

"My friend, Tobias, will be working with me. He's very competent at what he does. I hope you don't mind if he helps out over the next couple of weeks?"

Although framed as a question, it sounded more like an order.

She shuddered inwardly. She'd met Tobias only recently. He seemed so like a younger version of Gerry, she'd have marked them for brothers, or cousins. They looked alike, dressed alike and sounded alike. And more than once she'd suspected he and Gerry were 'partners' in the romantic sense. But where Gerry merely made her feel uneasy, Tobias made her flesh crawl – though she couldn't put her finger on why.

Julia stood, returned Bird to his perch and moved with purpose to the front door. "I'll have to think about it, Gerry, and talk to my accountant. Can you give me a few days?"

From the surprised look on his face, she gathered Gerry assumed it'd be a done deal. He followed to the door and stood just a little too close. "Well, if you need to speak to the accountant, I suppose I can wait. I'll stop by in a couple of days with a solid offer."

She hesitated, unable to meet his probing gaze. "I—ah ... you'll need an equipment list and other details, and of course, a copy of the books before you can make an offer. How about I give you a call after I've spoken to the accountant?"

His eyes narrowed.

"All ... right," he conceded slowly before he reached into his breast pocket and extracted a business card. "Here, I don't think you have my home number. I'm taking a few days off so I won't be at the gallery. Call home, or the cell." He handed the card across, but held it a moment too long when she tried to take it, forcing her to look into his dark eyes. They held a warning that said succinctly: Don't make me wait.

Once he'd turned to go down the stairs, Julia allowed herself a small sigh of relief. Shutting the door firmly, she leaned against it.

Now what am I going to do?

The tension had her wound tighter than a spring, and the aura of Gerry's presence made the apartment seem oppressive and small. Going from room to room, she threw open every window then went to retrieve her purse and sunglasses. A walk around the park, and perhaps the indulgence of a cappuccino and a slice of cheesecake would clear her head and allow the place time to 'air out'.

*

When she returned, the long walk and the fresh air had done the trick. Her mood had lifted and the apartment seemed more like home again. By the time she'd finished her cheesecake, she decided she'd simply let her imagination get the better of her where Gerry was concerned. She'd check with Irene, of course, but surely all her misgivings about him were just a product of her overactive mind.

After all, Irene had proved a very sensible and reliable friend, and if she trusted Gerry, then he must be, indeed, trustworthy. *Right?*

The message light on her answering machine caught her attention. For a moment she feared it might be another call warning her off Seth – but what if it was a client?

She pressed the button and listened as the machine went through its rewind sequence before the message came on.

"Good afternoon, Julia. This is Seth … " Relieved, the tension flowed from her limbs as she leaned back against the dining table to hear Seth's message. " … I've just received the painting back from the framers and it's now hanging in the office. If you're not too busy later, why don't you come and take a look. I think you'll be very pleased. Call me – you have the number."

Although she didn't think it prudent to meet the lion in his den, she dearly wanted to see where her painting ended up. And maybe, just maybe, Seth could give her some impartial advice about her plan to sell the photographic business.

There was also the matter of saying 'goodbye' – to both Seth and the painting. For her own sanity, she knew she had to sever the relationship sooner rather than later. And that warning call had only served to firm her resolve.

She picked up the phone and dialed.

"Julia," his voice seemed to smile as he spoke, "I'm glad you got back to me. Can you come to see our pharaoh in his new home?"

Our pharaoh? Both her brows rose.

"I suppose so. I just need to finish up some wedding prints, then I'll be free."

"Excellent. Why don't I send a car for you in what—two … three hours?"

She glanced at the clock above the stove. Two thirty. "How about we split the difference and make it five o'clock. I'll find my own way there, if you just tell me the address."

"I wouldn't think of it. The chauffeur has little enough to do as it is – he'll welcome a job. Rick will be there at five. Oh, and dress for dinner – we can have a meal after."

"Dinner? That's not necessary."

"Ah, but I want to celebrate – and we do really need to talk."

Yes, they did.

"Okay, I guess I'll see you a little after five."

As she hung up, she realized her heart rate had doubled. She had two-and-a-half hours to find some control. With an inner sense of determination, she headed for the bedroom and threw open her wardrobe doors. She needed to find just the right outfit, one that subtly said 'cold, remote and unavailable'.

Seven

"The driver tipped his hat when I opened the door!"

"Who—Rick?" Seth asked as he ushered her into his plush office.

"Yes. I didn't think people did that anymore ... political correctness and all that."

The corners of his lips quirked. She didn't need to know, quite yet, that her life might be in danger and that he'd had Rick collect her for that very reason.

"I'm a strong believer in good, 'old-fashioned' service and I do choose my staff well as you must have realized when you met Carolynne."

Carolynne was his secretary. A tiny woman of about forty, she had dark skin, black eyes and a slight accent. "I found her during my last trip to New Orleans. She'd just lost her husband, and worked as a, what's it called?" he clicked his fingers while he thought, "a ... temp? while I stayed there for an extended period. She turned out such a good secretary I decided to keep her."

"She didn't mind relocating?"

"Oh, we had a stroke of luck there, Carolynne has a daughter down in Warwick. She really wanted to be closer to her, and, just quietly," he whispered next to Julia's ear as he closed the door, "she's met a man."

Smiling, Julia turned to survey his office. A broad sweep of tinted windows on the outer wall, gave a wonderful view of the river and suburbs beyond. Evening had just begun to close in and already a sprinkling of lights glittered below. Opposite the windows sat an imposing, hand-sculpted executive desk. The superb grain had been polished to a high gloss – literally, a work of art. She crossed the room, unable to suppress the urge to touch.

"Do you like it?" Seth asked, coming to stand behind her.

"Very much," she murmured, smoothing her fingertips along the edge. "Where'd you get it?"

"I saw one like it, only smaller, while passing through a town called Graham, in Texas. The artist lived nearby, so I commissioned this before I came home. He only uses timber from trees that 'die of natural causes' as he put it, so it took him nearly nine months to find the right piece of wood. But it was worth the wait."

Glancing around further, she noted the series of old black and white photographs of Egyptian archaeological digs that adorned the walls at regular intervals. Her painting of Tuthmosis was nowhere to be seen. "I thought you said the painting is here."

"Actually, after framing it became too big to fit in this office," he motioned to a door at the other end of the room, "I had to hang it in the boardroom. Shall we take a look?"

Julia followed him through a connecting door to the boardroom. As she entered and gazed up, the framed painting nearly took her breath away. Her hand flew to her chest in an unconscious attempt to hold back the rapid beat of her heart. "My God – what have you done?"

"You don't like it," he said in a pained whisper.

Where it had come from she couldn't have said, but a single tear broke free and trickled down her cheek. "It's magnificent," she said almost breathlessly.

At the centre of the wall sat her pharaoh, just as she'd seen him last. But the frame! How he'd managed it she didn't begin to know, but he'd had the entire area surrounding the painting rendered in golden stone, as if it had come straight from the walls of some ancient Egyptian temple. The hieroglyphs and cartouches were etched so perfectly, it appeared as if her pharaoh had gone home.

"What ... how?" She turned to Seth, unable to form the questions she wanted to ask.

"The writings tell Tuthmosis's life story–" he explained as he pointed to various sections, "–or some of it. This portion is from his *Annals*," Seth indicated the top of the frame, "and tells of how he conquered the warring peoples to the North and East to create the largest empire the world had seen."

Julia followed his finger as it traced downward, over the row of tiny priests all facing the east. "And this tells of his ascension as pharaoh, though he was not officially the heir."

She raised an eyebrow but didn't comment – had she read that somewhere? *Maybe it was in the catalogue.*

"This," Seth indicated the first of the cartouches which held bees and geese, a zigzagged line and other symbols, "is his full name ... the Egyptian kings had five, long-winded names, and this one," he pointed to the next, "was his Great Wife. I think the others are minor wives.

"On the other side, is the story of his love for the slave girl, the legend we spoke about that day at the museum. And these," he indicated pictures of the giant pharaoh, smiting rows of much smaller men, "also come from his many conquests. Tuthmosis led Egypt to rise to the height of its power."

"You know," she said solemnly, "my painting doesn't really belong in the middle of all that history."

"Why not?"

She shrugged. "I–I suppose ... because it's not authentic."

Seth laughed and moved to stand beside her. "Even though I'd like to think the reliefs are real, they're only copies. Your painting is more authentic than any of the rest."

She spun about in surprise. "How can you possibly say that?"

His eyes roved over every aspect of her face before he answered. "How? That's easy. Your painting was born of a connection with the man, the god, for whom the statue was made. I can't explain why, or how I know this ... but I am certain Tuthmosis reached across time to catch hold of your heart as you painted him. I see it in those beautiful, green eyes every time you look at him. I felt it in your skin when you touched his face at the museum." He reached out and placed his fingertips on her cheek, echoing the motion they'd shared that day at the museum. "Unlike his carved face, your skin is warm. But it's just as smooth and compelling."

He took a small step closer and she held her breath. "Each time I'm with you, I have an overwhelming desire to touch you like this." Slowly, gently, his fingers slid downward and under her jaw to graze the pulse at her throat and her whole body seemed to leap in reaction. "As crazy as it might sound, this feels familiar – almost as if we've done this before. Do you feel it, too?"

Julia jumped back as if stung. She turned away and leaned against the table as she tried to catch her breath. His words made no sense – she didn't quite comprehend, and didn't want to. She didn't dare admit aloud the words that hung on the very edge of her memory. Like one of her overly dramatic dreams suddenly bursting to life, she saw, in her mind's eye, the man beside her naked from the waist up, except for a beaded golden collar, his smooth face, his eyes accented with kohl and green paint. She saw his head shrouded by a strange blue and gold striped scarf and a long, plaited, false beard, strapped to his chin with fine thonging.

The image made her dizzy and she swayed where she stood.

Seth gripped her shoulders and studied her face. "What is it, Julia? What did you just see?"

Averting her gaze, she straightened. "What makes you think I saw anything?" she replied, grappling for self-command, though her insides were quaking.

For a long second, he watched her. Then some of the tension seemed to drain from him. "Come, sit. I think it is time to tell you a story."

She hesitated, but when he smiled with tender reassurance, she admitted to herself that she'd probably follow him anywhere he asked – so welcoming was the light in his eyes.

When she sat by his side on a long burgundy couch, he took her hand and massaged her palm with his fingertips. "Promise me you won't think I'm insane, or run away until I've told you everything. Then, if you don't believe me, you can leave and never come back if that's what you want."

Julia leaned away a little and narrowed her gaze so she could see his face, measure his intent. But his face appeared so open and honest – almost vulnerable; the least she could do was hear him out. "All right … I'm listening."

"Thank you." He sat back and stared at the painting for several minutes before he began to speak.

"When I was fourteen years old my father took me back to Egypt to visit some of my family. I didn't really want to go; I'd lived in San Francisco so long I barely remembered any of those people. But my father said my destiny remained tied to our homeland and I owed it to my ancestors to learn of my heritage. So, grudgingly, I went along.

"One of my uncles, Salman, is a priest in the Coptic Church in my home town. One day, when we were visiting, he took me into the small library at the back of his church and showed me a whole lot of books and scrolls which contained translations from the walls of ancient tombs in the valley of the kings, and also some transcripts from writings that were destroyed by tomb robbers and early archaeologists." Seth's eyes glazed as if his mind was far away, lost in memory.

"Anyway, he showed me the books and scrolls, but they were all written in Demotic or Latin or Greek so they were just a whole lot of scribble to me, but he insisted on reading a few passages, saying they were important because they were about my family.

"I admit, at fourteen, I wasn't particularly interested in some musty old books but Uncle Salman appeared to think it imperative I know, so I listened as he read them in his broken English. He told me several stories, but this is the one I remember because it was a mystery about love and betrayal.

"It was an episode in the life of Tuthmosis, 'the greatest of the Egyptian kings,'" so Uncle Salman explained. He also said Tuthmosis was my ancestor. I don't know why he thought this, but he seemed so earnest, I believed him."

"How could he possibly know? The Pharaohs lived thousands of years ago," Julia uttered with disbelief.

"I'm not sure. I do know the priests of the local church prided themselves as great scholars, and kept written records from the time of St. Anthony. They translated scrolls and took down oral traditions, but I think they kept most of their records secret because in the early days the church in Rome often charged the priests with heresy. There were many sects and factions and it was dangerous to be on the wrong side of the most powerful group. Pre-christian histories were usually viewed as heretical."

Seth took her hand, tucked her arm under his and threaded his fingers through hers, gently forcing Julia to lean closer to him. It surprised her how comfortable and 'right' it felt.

His head eased onto the back of the couch and he closed his eyes, which allowed Julia to study his face while he spoke. He had a strong face, with a powerful, angular jaw; the arch of each of his black brows, clean and well defined. A ribbon of sensual warmth unfurled in her belly as she gazed at him. She knew his full mouth was soft, it had already left an indelible imprint upon her mind; her breath caught as the unbidden memory sent darts of fire through her belly.

Seth's eyes sprang open and he turned his head to smile down at her. His amber eyes became heated and welcoming – letting her know he was not only aware of her physical reactions, but her thoughts as well.

Her cheeks heated and she looked away.

"One of the stories he told me during the weeks I stayed there," he continued as if nothing had just passed between them, "was about the slave girl Tuthmosis fell in love with. There is much more to the story than I said at the museum. I don't know who she was – her name is lost, but my uncle thought her most likely the daughter of a minor prince of the conquered 'Retennu' peoples. She'd been brought back to Thebes as a hostage slave, but Tuthmosis supposedly freed her when she proved her allegiance, and later, her love."

Julia's pulse quickened as something in her mind seemed to click into place. The story had a familiar ring that she couldn't deny.

"Something happened to her shortly after they fell in love. My uncle seemed to think she was kidnapped or perhaps murdered by one of the few survivors of Tuthmosis's first campaign in Syria. Another version suggests she died at the hand of one of the royal wives. All the stories are vague on details, but Uncle Salman did say Tuthmosis swore to find her again, even if it took an eternity to do so. There's no record that he ever did."

"That's so sad. And sweet," Julia whispered, wondering what it would be like to be loved so deeply.

Seth's grip on her hand tightened for a second, then relaxed.

"Yes it is. But that isn't the end of it. According to my uncle, there are writings hidden in the church, which tell of similar stories occurring fairly regularly throughout my family's history – right up to present day. Every time the head of my family, usually the eldest son, finds the woman he loves beyond all else, his soul mate, she is stolen away or dies. And though he tries to protect her, by the time he learns it's the curse, it is already too late to prevent it happening again."

Julia looked up quizzically at Seth's face. "A family curse? You're kidding me!"

Slowly, he shook his head from side to side. "Not at all. My great, great grandfather is said to have lost his first wife only days after the wedding when a crazed cousin brutally raped her – she died of infection."

"But that could just be a coincidence." Julia ventured.

"Maybe. But there is also the story from around 1760 of a young bride who was poisoned by her stepsister. They say the stepsister was jealous of the girl's beauty and wanted to marry her intended, but another version says a political rival orchestrated the deed in an attempt to seize power in their province."

Julia smiled. "I'm sure most families can find similar events in their own backgrounds if they search hard enough."

"That is probably true," he stood and walked toward the painting as if it absorbed all his attention, "but I have other evidence. Many stories. And there are signs."

Standing, Julia joined him alongside the desk and watched the play of thoughts as they crossed his face. She was almost too frightened to ask the obvious question. "Signs?"

He turned to her and his expression held something she found completely unreadable. "Yes – signs. Unmistakable signs.

"The first is that the woman is often an artist of some kind – she makes beautiful things with her hands."

She knew he heard her sudden intake of breath, but a sad half-smile was his only response.

"Both the church back home and my grandfather's house are filled with relics and artifacts, paintings, drawings and quilts, or jewelry and small sculptures – the art of all the women lost to our family. All beautifully rendered by master artists, not the craftsmanship of amateurs.

"And then there's the dreams, the nightmares."

Julia spun toward him, her eyes wide with alarm.

"Dreams?" she begged in a thready voice.

He nodded and stepped closer. "Tell me, Julia, have you been having any strange dreams lately?"

"Me?" she shook her head in vehement denial. "Why would you think I've been having dreams?"

Taking both her hands Seth drew her into his arms, then lifted her chin when she tried to evade his probing gaze. Fire flashed from his eyes, challenging her to deny it again.

"Why?" he whispered. "That's easy – I've seen the haunted look you get sometimes when you see him, especially when we were at the exhibit. Your eyes betray the hundreds of question you want to ask, the confusion you obviously feel.

"And then there's the fact that I'm falling in love with you."

Her heart stilled and she clenched her eyes shut. No. She didn't hear him say what he just said. She couldn't have!

Wrenching herself from his arms, she fled to stand by the window and stare out at the darkening sky. The traffic on the street below looked like a glowing snake, slithering between the buildings.

"You can't honestly mean that."

She nearly jumped from her skin when she felt him right behind her.

"Why not?"

Lifting her head, she saw their reflections in the glass – him so tall and strong, almost regal in his bearing; alongside, she appeared small and insignificant.

"We met only weeks ago – you barely know me. You've kissed me a couple of times. How could you possibly fall in love so easily?" She turned to face him. "It doesn't happen that way."

His answering smile reminded her of when, during childhood, her father indulged her girlish delusions.

"It is said that when soul mates meet, it takes a mere glance."

The air in the room suddenly seemed thin. She backed up a step, trying to find the space to breathe. "You're just trying to fulfil the story your uncle told you. My painting probably gave you the idea."

"Do you truly believe that, Julia?"

She took another step back, needing to increase the gap. Seth inched forward, following, his eyes fixed on hers in absolute concentration like a stalking predator.

The table halted her escape. She held up her hand, motioning for him to stop. "This whole thing is preposterous. If you want to sleep with me, just say so. You don't have to make up elaborate stories to seduce me."

His smile broadened. "If I'd simply wanted to seduce you, we would have slept together before this moment. You know it, just as I know it, so don't bother with meaningless denials.

"We belong together. And, if Uncle Salman is right, then the curse is also upon us. Which means I must protect you from the danger that will no doubt threaten. Soon."

That word.

Again she shook her head. "No – you can't honestly think my life is in danger. That's crazy!" Even as she said the words the voice from the answering machine rose in her mind like a wail.

She looked up sharply. Could it be true? Could their lives really be in danger?

"What is it – something's happened, hasn't it?" He leaned closer, bracing his arms either side of her on the desk as if the mere weight of his presence could protect her.

Averting her face, she pushed at his arm to force him to give her the space to breathe. "It's probably nothing – just a prank." She glanced out the window and hesitated. Chances were the message wasn't even meant for her.

"Tell me."

With a sigh she faced him. "Someone left a nasty message on my answering machine."

"What did the message say?"

"It just warned me not to see 'him' again. The voice didn't say who."

"Was that all?" She felt anger seething in Seth's voice though he spoke calmly enough.

"No. The voice threatened that if I didn't do as it said, I'd pay."

"Did the voice use your name?"

"No. Like I said – it's probably just a prank." She tried to sound convincing but she knew she failed miserably.

"Have you still got the tape? I can have it analyzed within a day or two." He reached into his pocket and retrieved his cell phone and began to dial.

Julia put her hand over his in an attempt to stop him. "You can't – I erased it."

He let out an expletive before he shoved it back in his pocket. "Was it a man's voice? Did you recognize it?"

"I couldn't tell if it was a man or a woman – it sounded low and gravelly," she shrugged. "It could've been kids larking about."

"I doubt it." Again he retrieved the phone and pressed a button. "We'll test the chip anyway – it's marvellous what the techs can do these days. It might give us a clue as to who our enemies are."

He turned away from her and spoke in quiet tones. When he faced her again the thrust of his jaw seemed less rigid. "All organized. Now we'll–"

Suddenly she felt swamped ... that sick, hollow feeling she'd felt back in Australia when she first realized the stalker had been spying on her overwhelmed her in a familiar wave of nausea. She refused to believe it. Not again.

"No." She turned away and headed for the door, picking up her purse as she passed the board table. "I'm sorry about dinner but I can't stay." When her eyes darted up to see her pharaoh, her heart skipped. "The frame looks beautiful. Goodbye, Seth."

She raced past Carolynne's desk and made for the elevators without a backward glance.

Seth let her go. He didn't want to leave her unguarded, but he also knew she'd need time to sort through all he'd said. He'd have Rick keep a close eye on her until she'd had enough time to acknowledge the truth.

He stood in an alcove between the two offices and waited until she disappeared behind the elevator's sliding doors. Earlier, when he'd planned their meeting, he wasn't sure how she'd handle what he had to tell her. Yet, it was imperative she be warned. He didn't know the identity of their enemy and couldn't begin searching him or her out until Julia knew of the danger and could understand the actions he might be forced to take.

From the moment he'd first seen her, he'd known, deep inside, Julia was the one. And every meeting since only confirmed that notion. When he'd mentioned the dreams, her reaction answered the last remaining question in his mind. He just hoped, this time, they'd both be prepared to defeat their unknown enemy.

Carolynne entered the office with a steaming cup in hand.

"You look like you might need this, Boss."

Deep in thought, Seth barely acknowledged her statement, taking hold of the cup like an automaton.

Carolynne waved a piece of paper in front of his eyes, forcing him to snap out of his reverie.

"What?"

"Your manners have taken a nosedive tonight, Boss. I guess this Julia must be special."

For the first time since she'd entered his office, he turned to Carolynne. "Sorry, just preoccupied. What did you want?"

She waved the sheet again. "This. An email from your father – he's asking for a progress report on your cousin Jamal. It seems the new Philippines branch is nearing completion and they want him to be ready to take over the reins in about sixteen weeks."

Unable to suppress a groan, Seth took the missive and read it before rubbing his temple with a sigh. It was what he'd been dreading.

Jamal had dogged his every step in the office for more than six months and as far as Seth was concerned, the man just wasn't cut out for a life in international banking and brokering. Oh, he'd adequately performed every task Seth set, and seemed to understand the protocols necessary to make CEO, but the man had no flair, no intuition and he didn't seem to have the kind of investment eye needed to deal with the bigger clients. Nor could he speak effectively at board meetings. Jamal might have had a first rate education in economics and business administration, but in practice his work and ideas remained pedestrian at best. The man's heart just wasn't in it.

Seth nearly flinched to remember that he'd been forced to let Jamal take over while he made a lightning visit to London a few months back. Poor Carolynne – he'd coerced her to act the spy, watching Jamal's every move and he'd made her promise on her daughter's life that she would only hand over the papers granting Jamal his power of attorney if Seth died in an accident. He was so relieved when he returned to find that the papers still sat, untouched, in his safe.

But all that aside, the other more alarming problem was the fact that Jamal took the freedoms he found in this country to be a license for uncontrolled hedonism. Several times Seth had been forced to rescue his drunken cousin from seedy New York nightclubs after the fool's wallet and credit cards were stolen and he couldn't pay the bar tab. On another occasion he'd had to pay off a prostitute's strong man who'd threatened to castrate Jamal. The night he'd first seen Julia's painting, he'd been nursing injuries sustained while he and Rick rescued his reckless cousin from a dispute after an illegal game of fan tan in Chinatown.

And, each time, Jamal acted as if it was all just a bit of a lark.

To make matters worse, when he'd tried to subtly point out to his cousin that his behavior had the potential to ruin his burgeoning career, Jamal lashed out, claiming Seth was a boring snob – jealous because he didn't know how to have a good time.

In the end, Seth had read him the riot act, and, for the past fortnight or so, Jamal appeared to be behaving himself. How long it would last was anyone's guess.

It'll be a helluva long sixteen weeks.

Seth shook his head. He really didn't know what to do about his cousin.

"Thanks, Carolynne," he said, as he folded the paper and stuck it in his breast pocket. "Why don't you go home? You've been working too hard, lately."

After glancing at her watch, she smiled. "Yeah, I will. Trevor will be picking me up downstairs in a minute or two. Goodnight, Boss."

Carolynne spun about. "Oh, I nearly forgot – Hannah El-Safadi rang. Twice. She is eager to talk to you – said it was very important."

He didn't try to his grimace. Right now she was the last woman he wanted to see.

"I'll call her in the morning. Thanks, Carolynne."

*

On the street below, the man sat in his car smirking to himself. He felt just like an actor on a stake out in one of those old FBI movies.

Yeah, a stake out, he thought.

He supposed he should be wearing a hat and reading a newspaper, but it was almost dark, so he knew that'd be stupid.

The binoculars hadn't really helped much, but he'd seen the shadows moving back and forth in the office upstairs a short while ago. They'd stopped now, so he'd just have to sit it out and wait.

Scant seconds passed before the woman came running out of the building. He swallowed down his surprise and quickly ducked his head. Whatever'd happened up there, she didn't seem too happy. Well, that was good, if she was angry she'd play right into their hands. He just wished he could grab her now and be done with it. But there were still some things that needed to be accomplished before they could go into the final phase. Everything needed to be in place.

A taxi pulled up in time to mask the sound of his car's engine as it roared to life.

He watched her climb into the back seat of the cab – he hoped she intended heading straight home, he didn't fancy spending the night driving around the city.

A few minutes later, after easing his car into a vacant space across the street from her apartment, he picked up his cell phone.

"It's me ... yeah, she appears all locked up for the night ... okay, I'll wait another hour or two, just to be sure she's staying in ... okay ... I'll see you then."

He flipped the device closed and slipped it into his pocket before he slid down in the seat and pretended to go to sleep. All the while he kept one eye focused on the middle windows on the second floor. A good hour after the lights came on, all but the room he knew was the bedroom, went out again. And after another short while, that room went dark as well. When she didn't emerge from the building, he guessed she'd decided on an early night.

He sat another fifteen minutes, before he started the car and drove off toward his rendezvous.

When he pulled up outside the multicolored lights in the windows made it seem a fantasyland instead of a suburban house. The clairvoyant greeted him at the door wearing a bright orange translucent gown. Backlit from the doorway, he could see the outline of her body. She oozed sensuality and he knew, from the way she looked at him at times, that he could have her if he wanted her, despite her preoccupation with Almose.

"Welcome," she smiled as she spoke, and warmth surged up his spine. Yes, he thought he might just avail himself of what she had on offer. "Any news?"

"You're the clairvoyant, you tell me," he replied as he stepped past. Her musky scent wrapped around him.

With a throaty laugh she locked the door and directed him into the séance room.

Surprised to find the others already assembled, he nodded to each man as he took his usual place at the table. This time they joined hands without any urging. The ritual, one they'd become accustomed to over recent weeks, played out as it always did. He'd even come to accept that jab of pain that crossed his chest when the spirit came upon them. At least that what she said it was. He still wasn't so sure he believed any of it, but he had his plans and this coterie they'd formed allowed him to further those plans without the cost or effort he'd thought he needed.

His only worry was if the clairvoyant could see his true intent. She never suggested she knew, but she had been canny so far and he couldn't afford to discount the possibility.

His breathing fell easily into the rhythm they'd learned since coming here and forming their pact. His head swam with the energy that seemed to fill the room. The temperature rose and the air became thick, as if he'd entered a steamless sauna.

"Let the spirit enter," she whispered as the candle flames began their dance. "Spirit knows your desires. Spirit knows all your secret dreams. Spirit will reward your efforts in ways you'd dare not imagine."

The tenor of the air changed, a sudden gust of wind flashed through the room, snuffing the candles at the same moment as the slash of pain cut through him. Stronger this time. Their clasped hands sprang apart. He could barely catch his breath as the burning sensation dug deep. It was almost as if a hot knife twisted in his chest.

In the background he heard the groans of the others, though they sounded far away and indistinct. He collapsed forward, has burning cheek savoring the coolness of the wooden surface.

"That was the last time," she whispered. "We are close. The fates have aligned the forces."

He opened his eyes and stared up at her face. If he didn't know better he'd have said she glowed, though the cynic in him was certain she'd somehow manufactured some special trick with the lights to create the effect.

Like the others, he gathered himself slowly and sat back in his chair.

"Please, get yourselves a glass of wine from the tray," she motioned to the sideboard that held wine and a platter of fruits and cheeses. "I'll give each of you a private reading in the other room before you leave."

Eight

Julia woke with a start. She hadn't intended to sleep – just lay down for five minutes to catch her breath.

When she arrived home she realized she'd lied to herself as well as Seth. Yes she'd dreamed. Many times. And though she only remembered snatches of those dreams, she knew there'd been more than a shred of truth in what he'd said. How much truth, was the question. Did she want to find out? Could she?

"Who are you really?" she said aloud, wishing, just once, that the picture could speak – tell her what to do.

Studying the photograph on her wall, she wondered what happened to her resolve. Didn't she promise herself that she'd take the picture down? Destroy it?

She marched across the room, determined to follow through, but as she reached up, a small voice seemed to whisper in the back of her mind, and a flash of something like a vision, filled her brain. For one long moment she stared at a flesh and blood man, wearing a strange linen kilt and a blue and gold, striped headdress. His face, the face in the photograph, and Seth's face, appeared to converge into one being. Motionless, she felt as if she teetered on the precipice of knowing something – something very important. The man, so much taller and stronger than her, lifted a hand as if beckoning. And though she wanted to step closer, her feet seemed leaden – too heavy to move.

"What do you want?" she begged with her mind, her lips as immobile as her feet.

The pharaoh smiled, then murmured directly into her thoughts, "Don't trust him. Wait for me – I vow to save you."

Who shouldn't I trust? Seth? Someone else?

Slowly, the image began to fade ... and with a sudden jerk, Julia sprang upright.

Tears filled her eyes when she acknowledged this, too, was a dream.

"I'm going insane," she cried aloud, as she held her forehead and squeezed her eyes tightly shut.

The phone jangled and Bird began to squawk in response, and for one quivering moment she thought she might collapse into a blubbering heap. But she couldn't allow it. She was stronger than that and had been for a long time.

Ever since she'd escaped her stalker she'd been building strength and confidence. It had taken a time and lots of encouragement from Irene – but now she went days, sometimes weeks, without seeing that flash of *him* outside her window, without feeling that hollow fear that had pursued her once she realized he'd been watching her for months, perhaps years.

Breathing very deeply, she marshaled her thoughts, opened her eyes and picked up the phone.

"Have you spoken to your accountant?" The question sounded almost harsh and it took a second for Julia to recognize Gerry's voice.

"Gerry? Why are you're calling so soon – I asked you to give me a couple of days."

A muffled expletive shot down the phone line. Julia frowned.

"Actually," he continued, his voice sweetly coaxing, "I had hoped you'd gotten the ball rolling. I've spoken to my business partner, and moved some funds ready to make the deal."

Partner? – he didn't mention anything about a partner earlier. Tobias?

Swallowing down a growl of frustration, Julia said, "Look, Gerry, I appreciate that you're in a hurry now you've got your sights set, however I won't be speaking to the accountant before tomorrow at the earliest."

"But I've got an offer written up – can't I drop it around to you now?"

Her eyes darted across to the clock above the stove. It read 9:30. Well and truly too late for doing business as far as she was concerned.

"I'd prefer not, Gerry. Drop it by tomorrow afternoon – or have it couriered across. I'll get back to you then."

She slammed the phone down with more force than she intended and started to walk away only to have it ring again. Backtracking, her heart began to hammer in her chest. Why didn't she just tell the guy to take a running leap?

Tearing the earpiece from its cradle, this time she did growl, "Look, Gerry, I really don't–"

"Julia?"

It wasn't Gerry.

Seth's smooth voice was edged with real concern. "Are you okay?"

She had to take a moment to quell her anxiety before she could speak. "Yes, I'm fine." She couldn't help but sigh.

"You don't sound fine – I'm coming over."

He hung up before she could say anything to deter him.

Now she really felt like crying. What was happening? Why were these men trying to run her life? Her well-ordered world had veered out of control again. It had taken her almost two years to stop jumping at shadows. Two years of hard-won independence. Two years to change her name, her appearance and her home. She'd found a place where she'd finally felt able to build a foundation – a career. And now everyone seemed intent on forcing her to do and say things that were completely out of character. And then there were the dreams – and the havoc they wrought.

Perhaps I really should see a therapist.

By the time Seth knocked on her door logic had reasserted itself in her mind. She'd showered, made a pot of herbal tea and calmed her irrational thoughts. Tiredness had taken its toll – that was all. A few good nights' sleep and she'd be back to her usual self. Gerry was just overeager.

It was only a business, for God's sake!

And Seth? – Seth merely had seduction in mind. Maybe his methods were more sophisticated than most men's, but she could see no other good reason for his tall stories. He could have his choice of beautiful women – why on earth would he be interested in a mousy little Aussie painter?

The message on her machine? – just a coincidence.

As to her dreams, well, they were easy to rationalize. After her absorption in the painting and what she'd read in the exhibit's catalogue, a fragment of something she'd learned many years ago had taken root within her fertile imagination. Seth's stories simply made it all loom larger in her mind. And presto, lots of vivid, ridiculous, dreams!

That was definitely all.

"You didn't have to drop everything and come over," she said without preamble as she swung the door wide.

Seth was dressed casually, in tight, black jeans and a loose white shirt. His hair, as usual, was caught in a tail at the back of his neck. A pirate, she thought – the only element missing was the hoop of gold hanging from his ear.

"Then why did you sound so distressed on the phone?"

"I wasn't distressed – what you heard was anger. I'm fine. Really."

"You didn't sound fine to me," he accused. "Why the anger?"

She sighed. "If you must know, Gerry van der Gelder is pressuring me to sell my photography business to him. When you rang, I assumed you were Gerry.

"So there was no need to race over here," she added.

Seth's amber gaze studied her face for a long minute before he came in and closed the door behind himself. He crossed his arms over his chest as he leaned against the wall. "Why is he pressuring you, Julia?"

She shrugged. "Beats me. I told Irene this afternoon that I might be interested in selling the photography business so I could concentrate on my painting. And then, of course, there's the Egypt trip."

"If you want to sell – what's the problem?"

Again she shrugged. "That's just it – I don't know. That business was my baby – I started it and nurtured it ... selling it to Gerry simply feels wrong, like I'm handing my only child over to someone I'm not sure I can trust." She turned away then spun back and looked up hesitantly. "Does that make any sense?"

"As a businessman, I'd say, if it feels wrong, don't do it. Gut instinct usually works for me." He walked over to Bird's perch and placed his forefinger against the parrot's chest. Bird immediately jumped onto Seth's hand and began to nibble at his thumb.

Traitor, she thought in disgust, though she didn't say the word out loud.

"I'd intended discussing the idea with you earlier tonight, but ... "

Returning Bird to his perch, Seth turned and raised an eyebrow. "But what?"

"Well – we sort of got distracted by other things. It doesn't really matter. I'm probably just being silly. Gerry's never done anything to make me think he shouldn't buy the business. He just makes me feel uncomfortable." She lifted her teacup toward him. "Do you want a cup of tea – it's peppermint?"

He nodded and followed her to the small kitchen area.

"I'll admit I don't like the man at all," Seth reached around her to lift a cup from the open cupboard above the sink, "I've met him only a few times, but he gives the impression he wants something – a real opportunist, and that day at the museum, he seemed almost angry."

"Do you think so? Angry? Why would he have been angry?" She shook her head in disbelief.

"Like I said at lunch, I think he's smitten. Perhaps he saw me as a rival for your affections?"

Her head whipped around so fast she nearly spilled tea all over the sideboard. "That's preposterous!"

"Why?"

"Because ... because he's never even hinted that he feels anything for me. To be honest, I thought he was gay – he's always with this friend of his, a guy named Tobias – never a woman."

"That might be because he has a great big crush on *you*."

"You can't be serious." She dropped her head and closed her eyes. "Oh, God. If I do sell to him, he wants us to work together for a couple of weeks until I hand over the business. Now I'm going to feel even more uncomfortable. You've got to be wrong."

Seth shook his head, a glint of mischief in his eyes. "As a man who has strong feelings himself, I'd be willing to bet I'm right. I saw the way he watched you. He had that hungry look."

"What hungry look–" a nervous little giggle bubbled up her throat, "–you're making this up, aren't you?"

He stepped closer, filling the space between them, warming it. "Not at all. It's the same hungry look that I probably get whenever I see you."

Her face heated instantly and she turned away. "Please, Seth. Don't say things like that."

With deliberateness, he placed his teacup down and reached around to lift her face until his gaze held hers captive. Gold clung to green until she felt her heart tremble.

"Did you think I'd let you walk away?" he asked, his gaze unrelenting.

"I–" Whatever she might have wanted to say, the words were lost as he bent to touch his lips to hers. As light as a feather his lower lip slid along hers – forcing a whispered moan from deep in her chest.

"You were saying?" he challenged softly. But he didn't let her answer. He took her mouth and stole her breath and wiped every thought from her mind save the feel of his lips and tongue as they wove a sensual spell around her. He was soft and warm and hard and compelling, all at the same time. As he drew her into his arms, she curved against him and the instant their bodies met, a fire ignited. She realized he not only told the truth about how he felt; her own body screamed its agreement. Her pulse thrummed as his hands wove a knowing path up her back until his fingers threaded their way into the thick hair at her nape. She clutched at the collar of his shirt, to steady herself as she fell headlong into a well of raw emotion.

A shirt button popped and danced across the bench top.

He broke contact long enough to give her a glowing smile, before he bent to lift her into his arms. As he carried her to the couch, he resumed his kiss, more heated, more passionate than anything she'd ever known. Yet at the same time, she felt a fleeting sense of *deja vu*, like they'd done this before – but she couldn't quite catch hold of the memory.

And she knew the truth in what he'd said – had known it all along, despite her denials. They did belong together.

With gentle hands, Seth laid her on the couch and sat beside her, lifting her hair until it fanned out over the cushion.

"You know, don't you," he murmured as he ran his thumb along her cheek.

Ripples of sensation followed his every touch, and though she wanted to answer him, her mouth couldn't quite form the words. Her eyes darted across to the photograph, then back to is face. Both seemed to glow.

"You remember *him–*" he said with certainty, "–you remember *me.*"

Julia wanted to deny it. They could not be the same man! It was too surreal, too unbelievable. Yet, no matter how illogical, acceptance made all the puzzle pieces fall into their rightful positions. All the snatches of her dreams made sense.

"I ... " There was nothing she could say.

Softly, he kissed her forehead and stroked her hair. "I remembered you. I loved you more than life, but somehow I lost you. I'm not sure how, or why. But together, if we try, we might just be able to figure it out and break the curse."

"How?"

Seth grinned and suddenly that look of mischief was back. "By loving each other."

Before she could protest, his fingertips slid downward, skimming the pulse at her throat. Every nerve stood to attention and she couldn't stop the shiver that coursed down her spine. Her eyes remained locked with his in an embrace that went beyond words but still said so much. Gave so much.

"This time," he whispered as he bent to place his lips over her heart, "this time, they won't win. This time we *will* be together."

With shaking hands she released the band that held his hair. The fine, ebony strands felt like warm silk as they slipped through her fingers and spread over her chest. He lifted his head, and for an instant, her mind's eye recalled her beautiful pharaoh in all his splendor, before Seth's questing mouth dragged her back into the here and now.

One by one, he undid the small pearl buttons of her blouse, placing wet kisses over the skin he revealed. His tongue slid into the cleft between her breasts, drawing a muffled groan from her. He made her ache, not with pain, but with wanting, and she realized no man had ever come close to awakening such need in her – and yet he'd barely touched her body.

What he had done was sear her soul.

Suddenly she understood. The magic existed in the joining of mind and spirit – something that was eternal and predestined, transcending all thought of time and bodies. Two halves, one being – soul mates.

"Come," he said as he stood. He held out his hands and helped her stand, then slid her blouse from her shoulders. It fluttered to floor with a quiet rasp.

With the same deliberation, Seth removed his own shirt. Julia swallowed. The man before her was the image of the one in her dream, but at the same time there existed a newness, a suggestion of discovery.

Broad and strong, as if sculpted from warm stone, the very sight of him made her breath quicken.

Adrenalin surged through her, heating and dampening, as he moved to her jeans. His knuckles grazed her belly as the button broke free, setting nerve endings aflame. The snap echoed in the pregnant silence of the room as he dropped to his knees and slid the denim over her legs. Butterfly kisses danced down her abdomen and thighs, and she thought her legs would surely buckle so gentle was his touch.

He stood and smiled and her insides seemed to melt.

Taking her hands, he drew them to the clasp of his belt. "Your turn," he murmured.

Her lower lip quivered with hesitation.

"It's okay," he reassured, caressing her cheek. He closed the space between them and held her tight, again taking her mouth with his. This kiss was different. Consuming and demanding, she had to fight to remember to breathe. His questing hands removed her bra then pulled her closer, flattening her breasts against his chest. The silky hair abraded her tender nipples; the sensation one of absolute bliss.

"Oh, God, I've come home," she whimpered, thinking out loud. She held his face and brought it down to initiate the kiss, saying 'thank you', though for what, she couldn't have said.

When he lifted her, she instinctively wrapped her legs around his waist, his belt buckle branding her inner thigh. Slowly, as if swaying to a silent waltz, he spun her in lazy circles until they reached her bedroom door, never once breaking the kiss. At the door he drew away and gently released her, lowering her until she stood on the carpeted floor.

He cupped her face in his broad hands and looked into her green eyes. "I once asked you if you believed in fate. Or reincarnation. Do you know the answer now?"

With only the barest hint of hesitation, she replied, "I think so."

"Then you understand what's happening here? – if we do this, if we cross the threshold, there'll be no turning back. It will be like taking a vow, the same vow we took eons ago but never quite fulfilled."

"I understand."

"Do you? It will mean never again being apart. It'll mean marriage, everything that entails and more – because if we choose to join completely – it will be *complete*. I'll accept no less. No holding back, no secrets, no separation – no space between us. Ever."

Julia's eyes closed at the enormity of what he asked, yet, deep in that all-knowing centre of her being, she realized it was what she wanted. More – it was her destiny. He was her destiny. She didn't notice the lone tear that broke free to sparkle as it tracked down her cheek.

Stepping closer, she took his hands and brought him one step at a time into her private sanctuary. "No space, no secrets." She stood on tiptoes and brushed his mouth with hers. "Ever," she whispered.

"I love you," he murmured as he lifted her to the bed. "I always have." He hooked his fingertips into the waistband of her panties and slipped them off, all the while staring at the vision before him. He wanted to cherish this moment, but at the same time his need to be part of her urged him on.

Moving to his jeans, he slid them over his hips and stepped out of them. The bed creaked as he lay down beside her.

He held a shaking hand to her lips, caressing the lower one with his thumb. "See what you do to me?"

Her eyes widened as she looked first at his hand, then lower. *"Oh. My."*

"Yes, indeed," he laughed, before reaching across to skim her hardened nipple. "And I'm not the only one."

Julia felt her cheeks burn and he gave another playful laugh before his mouth moved to cover her breast, teasing until she writhed and struggled away from the sweet torment. But he held her against his hard body, preventing her escape.

With his large hand splayed over her abdomen, he inched lower with agonizing slowness until she couldn't help but lift her hips in invitation. His tongue traced the lines of her thighs and tasted the soft flesh behind her knee.

"Please, stop," she begged. "I need you."

He looked up into her eyes, his face serious. "It's more than that, isn't it?"

"Yes," she breathed, "almost too much." Every touch brought her body so alive; like the flesh was being singed from her bones.

Using his elbows to keep the bulk of his weight from crushing her, he gradually slid up her body, kissing and tasting every place he could reach until he was poised above her. His black hair curtained their faces as if they hid in a world of their own. A flash of memory raced through her mind. But she couldn't hold onto it, Seth's gentle touch compelled her beyond all distraction.

A low groan was wrested from her throat as he slid into her and rested fully within her warmth.

"Dear god," she whimpered.

The feeling of wholeness, of completion, was almost shattering in its intensity.

"It's us," Seth said with a broad smile. "Only a short while ago you said there was no 'us.'" He lowered his lips until he tasted her tears. "But deep down, you knew, didn't you."

"I was scared," she admitted, her eyes drifting shut on a sigh as he began to move, slowly tilting his hips away, only to surge deeper. She caught her breath. "I didn't want to feel those emotions."

"And now?"

Her eyes sprang open as he pushed into her again. "Now I know I've been a fool." She wrapped her long legs around him, urging him even deeper.

His answering look signaled the time for talking was over.

Although he wanted to ease her into her ecstasy, the years of waiting for her to come to him left no room for controlled passion. He groaned as he ceased trying to fight the overwhelming sensations. She was so hot and wet and open to him, his body could no more deny that summons than it could cease to breathe. Her hands roamed restlessly over his back, pleading, coaxing, begging for completion. Each scrape of her nails, each moan she uttered, only drove him deeper and faster.

The eruption overcame her an instant before his began. She cried out his name then shattered in his arms as he was helplessly flung along in her wake. His need became so intense; he nearly crushed her as the final wave struck him.

*

Bastard!

The man sitting vigil in the street below let fly with another string of expletives and thumped the steering wheel in frustration as soon as they disappeared from view.

He'd been caught by surprise when Almose's car pulled up at the curb outside her apartment. He watched helplessly as the banker went inside – far too late to create a diversion.

And then the asshole has to go and screw her! She belonged to him – not that asshole! Now she would really pay.

From his vantage, the man could see everything that happened in her living room. The stupid bitch had no idea the odd lights she used when she painted, created vivid, larger-than-life silhouettes against the floor to ceiling blinds. So he knew when they were kissing. He saw Almose take off her clothes, saw when he carried her into the bedroom.

He didn't need to *see* any more.

Asshole!

She'd pay. They'd both pay. He allowed his mind to picture the various ways he'd make her beg. For years he'd thought of ways he'd make her come to him – but now she'd gone and given herself to that asshole banker, he'd make her come to him on her knees. Of that he was certain. She'd crawl to him.

The cruel mental images made him feel strong – he got hard just thinking about it. Cursing her, he slipped his hand inside his trousers to distract himself with the promise of her utter subjugation. Within seconds he cried out, shaking with anger as he tried to hold back the anguished rush of his premature release.

"Bitch!"

Even in that, she robbed him. Every time, she did it to him. He hated her.

Still panting, he scanned the neighborhood to check no one had seen or heard. Once satisfied the area was clear, he dropped his head back to catch his breath for a few moments, before finding an old t-shirt on the floor of the back seat to clean up the mess he'd made of himself.

He had to think. The other partners would not be pleased when they learned she'd slept with Almose. They'd assumed they had more time, but now they'd have to bump up their schedule. Christ! He didn't want to tell them – he'd be knee-deep in shit when they found out.

For a short while he toyed with the idea of keeping this to himself, but as fast as the thought came, he dismissed it. No. It wouldn't work. If Almose and his Julia'd had it off, then they'd be one step closer, which'd be too close for anyone's comfort.

He'd have to tell.

Rustling around in the glove box, he found a smoke and his lighter. When he'd lit the cigarette, he breathed in the polluted air as if it was a lifeline. He checked his watch. Nearly an hour since Almose'd turned up – maybe the asshole'd sleep the night. More hassle. He knew he should call and tell his partners the bad news, but a few hours wouldn't hurt, he decided, as he pulled out the flask of brandy he kept stashed under the seat in case of emergencies. Chugging back a big swallow, he groaned when it burned its way down his throat.

As he lifted the bottle to his lips again, he murmured, "Yeah, one shit of an emergency."

Nine

Seth wondered if his heart would ever stop thundering. Although it had been quite a while, he knew that making love had never left him this elated. He'd lost all conscious control as his emotions sent him blindly over the edge. He thought he'd prepared himself for the depth of feeling he'd experience. After all, his grandfather had told him many times what to expect. But his grandfather's words didn't come close. Every nerve, every muscle, every sinew of his being, seemed infused with her essence. He felt so calm, as if nothing in the world could disturb his peace, yet, at the same time, he felt so incredibly charged, like he could easily jump up and run a marathon.

All because of the incredible woman who slept beside him.

He looked across at Julia's face just as she began to stir. When her eyes fluttered open, he saw that almost all the color had left her irises – they were pale rings around massive black pupils that shone straight at him.

"Are you okay?" he asked, gently lifting her head until it rested on his shoulder. "I didn't hurt you, did I?" He stroked her arm absently as he spoke. "I got a bit carried away there."

The corners of Julia's lips twitched in a gentle half-smile. "No, you didn't hurt me. Shocked me a little, but hurt?— no." Her breath came out in a series of small shudders.

"I shocked you? How?"

She gave him a faraway look. "You know – you were there."

A loud bark of laughter erupted from deep in his chest. "God, I love you." He hugged her tight then rolled her over until she lay full-length on his body, before kissing her soundly.

For a long while they lay together, listening to each other breathe. Neither had the strength to move. Nothing could invade this idea of heaven.

When Julia appeared to have fallen deeply asleep, Seth carefully rolled her onto her back and eased off the bed. He covered her with the sheet and pressed a soft kiss to her brow. "Sweet dreams, babe."

After a quick toilet stop, he pulled on his jeans, went into the kitchen and made himself a cup of coffee. A raid of the cupboards yielded a muesli bar and a jar of pistachios – he suddenly had an appetite to rival a heavyweight boxer's.

In a way he felt incredibly relieved. He'd found her – he'd finally found her. All the uncertainty was over. But he also knew it was only the first hurdle. Now he had to protect her. From whom, or what, he didn't know. Yet.

And because they'd made love, their plight became all the more urgent. It was the reason his forefathers had never been able to break the curse. They'd always been too late to understand the danger. Once the commitment was made, whether by betrothal, or marriage, or simply making love, the outcome remained the same. As soon as the pact was sealed, doom followed almost immediately after.

He found his cell phone in his shirt pocket, unlocked it and punched in two numbers. Rick answered after three rings.

"Rick, it's time ... yes, do a full security sweep of the penthouse, then prepare the master bedroom for our guest. Oh, and have Steve prepare the second bedroom, Julia's going to need somewhere to paint ... I'll stay here tonight so give me a call when everything's ready and you can organize the move. Make sure you also screen the moving company very carefully, we can't afford any slip ups." He listened as Rick assured him everything was under control. "... yeah ... okay ... let me know if you hear or see anything amiss between now and then." Ending the call, he slipped the phone back into his pocket.

Just as he hung his shirt over the back of the kitchen chair, he heard Julia whimper in her sleep. He went to the door and watched her restless movements and wondered whether she dreamt about his ancestors. But a minute or two later she seemed to settle once again so he retreated to the living room to finish his coffee. Bird opened one eye and studied him before tucking his head under his wing to resume his nap. Bird would be very happy in his apartment, too, he mused.

When he'd rinsed his cup, Seth double-checked the lock on the front door, and each of the tall windows that opened onto her small balcony. Satisfied all was secure, he slipped off his jeans and crept back into bed. Julia wriggled closer to his warmth then sighed in her sleep.

With one arm wrapped around her, he let himself imagine what it'd be like to spend the rest of his nights this way, but he didn't have much chance to think about it – for the first time in as long as he could remember, he fell immediately into a deep and restful sleep.

*

The driver took the hairpin bend too fast and nearly lost control, the tires screeching like a scalded cat as the vehicle sluiced sideways on the wet road.

"Freakin' hell!" the man sitting in the passenger seat screamed. "Are you trying to kill us?"

The driver slowed the car and sneered. "D'you want to drive?"

The passenger let his head roll back on the headrest, closing his eyes against the glare of an oncoming car. "No – you drive. I'm too tense anyway. So you're positive he's still there?"

"How many times do I have to tell you? He went up and didn't come down – and they weren't having high tea up there, neither. Them blinds showed everything clear as crystal. Those two are bonking the night away as we speak," he added with a disgusted scowl, reliving the frustration he felt as he watched them disappear into the bedroom.

"Fucking banker!" the passenger growled. "Why didn't you do anything to stop it?"

"And what was I supposed to do? Huh? Tell me that! I couldn't go knockin' on the door, now could I?"

"Well, you could've rung or texted. Made up an emergency. The bank burning down or something!"

"Christ, you're an idiot sometimes – would you answer the phone when you're about to bonk the chick you got the hots for? Any man in his right mind'd let the call go to his message service – I know I would." In his mind's eye he pictured the moment when she would go down on her knees before him and beg – he won't be answering any phone then, that's for sure.

The passenger looked away and stared at the passing traffic. The bastard was right; they should have stopped Almose going there in the first place.

The car pulled into the suburban driveway and the driver killed the lights. The third member of their partnership already had the front door open, waiting.

"Took you long enough – hey," he said to the man who'd driven the car as he entered the house, "are you certain Almose is still there?"

"Christ, man. Like I told shit-for-brains here," he gestured at his black-haired accomplice with his thumb, "they're 'at it' big time. No doubt about it. I saw him go up. Huh! I even saw him get it up!" he sniggered, though his companions didn't appear to appreciate the joke. "When I left, not half an hour ago, his car still sat in the street out front of her apartment."

"She did say it was in the cards," he stated as a reminder.

The big man, who'd rented the house when they'd begun this endeavor, crossed the sparsely furnished room to a makeshift bar and grabbed a bottle of bourbon. He filled a shot glass and drank it straight down, before turning to offer the other two men a drink. After pouring both a healthy dose he refilled his own glass.

Calmer now, he sat on a plastic garden chair by the bar and scrubbed his face. "Well, this is it. Tomorrow's the day." He glanced across at the guy who drove the car. "Get back over there by dawn, we need to know where they go and what they do, so we can cement the plan. If he does what I expect and takes her to his place, it should be easy." To the third man he said, "Be ready when I give the signal."

"I'll get things set at my end. Let me know as soon as they make a move." He stood, preparing to leave.

The driver followed suit. "I'm gonna grab a burger and then go get a coupla' hours shut-eye. One of you'd better ring me about five, just to make sure I'm awake. That should be enough time to get back over there."

The big man nodded. "Just make sure your phone is juiced up."

"Yeah, yeah," the driver gave a wave of dismissal and let himself out.

He didn't really intend heading home – he'd go back and watch in case Almose leaves, then he'd go up to her apartment and get what he'd been waiting for all these years.

The other two didn't have any idea how long he'd watched her – how he'd planned. He'd told them a little, of course, but not all of it. They thought they were in charge – but he'd have her first, even if he had to kill the pair of them. And the clairvoyant.

Bet she wouldn't see that in her bloody cards!

*

Twice during the course of the night, Julia stirred in his arms. Once, she stretched like a contented cat and reached for him, mumbling words of love and bringing him instantly aroused. He was half inside her before she came fully awake, but the moment she opened her eyes and recognized him, she smiled and drew him to complete her. Neither said a word, though their eyes communicated with such eloquence, he felt as if he'd spent his entire life beside this woman.

Their loving was slow and sweet and filled with gentleness. His hands moved over her in the softest of caresses – learning her, while his lips tasted every inch of skin he touched. And when the moment of rapture finally came their eyes met and held, unwavering, as the internal fires raged. Tears sparkled down her cheeks and he traced their saltiness with his tongue. She smiled up at him, holding him close as if she would be satisfied to remain in his arms for the rest of eternity. This once, he thought in quiet desperation, he truly wished it would be so. He buried his face in the warm hollow of her throat and fell asleep cradled in her arms.

Later, just before the first light of dawn crept into the room, she began to thrash about as if she fought a demon no one else could see. Seth held her in his embrace, protecting her as she rode out the turmoil, afraid to wake her in the midst of such distress. He just hoped if she dreamt of his ancestor, she would remember something that would help them form a defense in this lifetime.

When she settled again, he allowed himself to relax as well. They were safe for the time being. But if he was right, the days ahead would require a great deal of concentration; he needed whatever sleep he could get.

*

Julia stretched languidly then glanced over Seth's shoulder at the clock. Six fifteen. She rose up on one elbow and allowed herself the luxury of watching him sleep. One arm was thrown above his head and he snored faintly. His face appeared so young when he wasn't frowning at her. She reached across and lifted the strands of hair that had fallen across his forehead, before placing a gentle kiss on his shoulder.

As she breathed in the scent of him, the thought struck her that not once during the course of the night, did she think about her stalker. For two long years she'd been terrified that that animal had ruined any hope that she could make love without fear, ever again. Yet, when the right man had come along – loving him had been so natural, and so easy, nothing could mar it. She wanted to wake Seth and thank him for releasing her from the emotional prison she'd been living in, but that would have meant explaining and she didn't want to soil last night's intimacy with sordid memories that should simply be buried with the past.

She allowed herself the pleasure of running her fingertips over Seth's flank, marveling at his strong male beauty.

"Cat's tongues and croissants for breakfast, I think," she murmured to herself with delight as she carefully extricated herself from the bedclothes. At the door, she lifted her jeans and a t-shirt from the chair, and tiptoed out into the living room.

As she dressed, she noticed the coffee cup on the sink and wondered when Seth had gotten out of bed. She couldn't recall him leaving her.

As she entered the living room her eyes automatically sought out the photo of her pharaoh and the unwanted memory of her dream came crashing back. It began as something incredibly beautiful. Her pharaoh had finally found his true love. Their coming together seemed almost magical, just like her and Seth.

She smiled to herself – *exactly like her and Seth.*

But all too soon, the dream turned violent. Julia felt a coldness growing in the pit of her stomach, a sickly feeling that increased as the memories became more vivid.

Fear rose up in her breast when she saw the men. There were two, but one stayed in the shadows, just watching. Her brother. It made no sense!

The other man, dark and threatening, ripped her gown from her so she stood small and naked and powerless. He'd toyed with her, showing no shred of humanity and he seemed to relish her feeble attempts at escape.

Julia's heart began to hammer. She was there and watching at the same time.

The torturer showed no mercy, lashing her again and again with a honey-drenched whip before working himself into a sexual frenzy and emptying himself onto her collapsed body.

Suddenly her stalker's face loomed large in her mind. *Could he be reborn as well?*

The blood. It pooled on the floor and streaked the wall. Julia could almost smell it, even now.

Dear God. The futility of the poor girl's struggles. Julia experienced it all, her own pulse raced and she wanted to scream. Each stroke of the whip stung her skin, just as it did the girl's.

Julia shook in horror that the girl's own brother could sit by and watch his friend's savagery. The girl begged and pleaded but he just stared at her as if bemused.

Julia felt the girl's utter anguish, the sense of betrayal and ultimate desolation until unconsciousness finally put her beyond the brutality.

A sudden flash of recognition tore her thoughts in a different direction – images of another woman, a lesser queen with harsh features and an ugly sneer, invaded Julia's mind. The woman's venom was so palpable Julia almost stepped back as the woman's image reared at her like a cobra.

Paralyzed, Julia hugged at the hollow ache within herself as she recalled it all. She lived everything as if it actually happened to her. Could Seth be right? Could she be that tragic soul, reincarnated?

Tears flowed down her face as she relived all those tangled emotions and she didn't even notice when Seth, wrapped only in a bath towel, came up from behind and took her in his arms. She shuddered.

"It's okay, babe, I'm here," he whispered as her picked her up and carried her to the couch. He settled her on his lap and gently stroked her brow until she began to regain composure. "Tell me what you saw."

"Hell, Seth–" she shook her head and swallowed hard, trying to block out the images, but they were so relentless she thought she would suffocate under the weight of the girl's terror.

It took quite some time before she felt able to speak, but when she did, she poured out the entire story. As she spoke, many pieces of the ancient puzzle fell into place. Some pieces, Seth already knew, but others came as quite a surprise. He'd always suspected that the slave girl had been tortured or murdered. But her brother's involvement shocked him to the core.

"Can you remember anything else?" Seth asked once she'd fallen silent. "Anything that might help us know who these people are in this life?"

Closing her eyes, she thought hard but nobody she knew even remotely reminded of any of the characters in her dream. "No – nothing. Maybe it isn't true – maybe my mind has just conjured up the whole thing," she offered hopefully, but the look on Seth's face told her what he thought of that idea.

"I wish to god, you're right. But I know the curse is real. And I know what we must do."

Julia sat upright and stared at him through tear-filled eyes. "What do you mean?"

"Rick has already been alerted. You're moving into my apartment today – I don't intend to let you out of my sight until I'm certain the danger is over."

She stiffened. "No – that's ridiculous. I'm not reorganizing my life, overnight, on the strength of one of my stupid dreams. What if all of this is just a product of my overly fertile imagination?"

Seth sighed. "You know that isn't true – your life is under threat and you know it. It's the only way I can protect you."

"Look," she said in a tone she hoped conveyed a sense of reason, "I understand how you feel, but can't we just take a few days to think about this? There's so much to do, and I'm still not certain I believe the dreams are anything more than vivid fantasies. Nobody has actually threatened me."

When she evaded his eyes he placed his index finger under her chin and drew her closer. "How can you say that after what happened last night? And don't forget the message on your answer machine. We don't have time to make plans. The moment we committed ourselves, we also brought the danger closer. We haven't got days – probably not even hours."

"Surely it's not that urgent."

"I'm afraid it is – they could be outside right now, waiting."

Her brow furrowed. "Don't you think you're being a bit melodramatic?"

"Not if you knew my family history – I just told you about a couple of cases. Every time, every woman, has died or disappeared since before written history. Documents dating back to the time of Christ describe how they were tortured and raped. Some were murdered. Others just vanished, but in the end it is always the same."

He gripped her shoulders and gently squeezed.

"Look, I promise, when we get to my place you can read the records for yourself if you want – but please, even if you do it just to humor me, come to my place where I can protect you."

"What about Bird? And my painting?"

"All taken care of. The penthouse has an atrium with a large garden, I'm sure Bird will be very happy there, and I have an unused bedroom that has floor to ceiling windows along an entire wall – a perfect artist's studio if ever I've seen one."

She swallowed – he had an answer to every argument she could think up. "Am I to become a prisoner like the girl in my dream?"

He pulled her to him and kissed her deeply. The hot, wet sweep of his tongue almost made her forget her question. Almost. When he broke the kiss she threw him a playful glare.

"Well?"

"Well what?" he replied, feigning ignorance.

"Are you planning to hold me prisoner?"

"Not at all – you'll be allowed to leave whenever you want, just so long as Rick or I go along."

Julia rubbed her eyes, hardly able to believe he was really serious about this. In many ways it smacked of a second rate movie.

"Even if everything you've told me is true, what if it takes years to find these people? And what if they don't come after us at all? Are we going to spend our entire lives locked up in your apartment?"

He laughed and hugged her close. "The idea certainly has a lot to recommend it."

Before she could object, his face became deadly serious. He flicked her hair over her shoulder and stroked the silky strands. "If they follow the usual pattern, we'll know soon enough. Now, let's think about who we can put on our list of suspects?"

"You're assuming we know them at all – what if they're perfect strangers?"

Taking her hand, he threaded their fingers. "How about we take it one step at a time. First the people we know. Then, if we can't come up with anybody, we'll look further afield. Okay?"

With a nod, she set about mentally listing all her friends and associates. Despite the clues in her dream, she knew her brother wasn't part of it. He was one of the gentlest souls on earth and had no reason at all to want to hurt her. The same could be said for her parents – plus they were all half way across the world.

Irene was her closest friend here in Boston – had been for nearly two years, and although she seemed a little offbeat at times, she didn't have a nasty bone in her body.

One by one she ticked off various acquaintances, regular photographic customers and gallery owners. Eventually, she could come up with only one name. But, and it was a big but, she really had no reason to assume he had any involvement, other than an uncomfortable gut feeling.

"So?" Seth said, breaking into her musings, "have you thought of anyone?"

With a slow shake of her head, she sighed. "In all honesty, the only person I can even remotely think of is Gerry – and then it's just because he gives me a creepy feeling." She couldn't say whether he truly resembled one of the men in her dream.

"Hmmm. I've had him investigated – Rick says he checks out. Apart from his *avant garde* friends, and his habit of spending his nights at exclusive New York nightclubs, there's nothing in his background to say he could be involved," he hugged her tighter and thought for another minute, before continuing, "which can only mean that they are probably business associates of mine. I've had dealings with any number of people over the years – and in finance, it's easy to make enemies – even ones you don't know about.

"I'm sorry, babe," he rested his forehead on hers and let out a long, low sigh, "it looks like this is all my fault."

She knew she should have told him about her stalker two years ago. But what could she say? She didn't know who the man was, even back then. Besides, she'd left him behind in Australia, a long time ago. There is no way he could be tied to any of this.

"Nuh-uh," she placed her fingertip over his lips, "don't talk like that – we're in this together and we'll get through it together." She smiled and pressed her lips lightly to his. "So, I guess, if you're going to take me prisoner, we'd better get on with it." She stood and held her wrists out before him. "Are you going to tie me up?" she asked, her green/gray eyes twinkling with mischief.

Seth caught her hands and dragged her back down until she lay sprawled across his chest. "Only after you have your evil way with me"

Julia squealed as he began tickling her midriff and seeking out the bare flesh beneath her clothes. An instant later, she stilled as his open mouth found hers and he plunged his tongue deep inside. His hands sought her breasts and feasted.

"I think I'm already your prisoner," she murmured as he undid the snap of her jeans and began sliding them down her thighs.

"I was yours from the moment I laid eyes on you," he replied.

She kicked her jeans aside then unhooked his towel to allow him his freedom. Sitting astride his hips, she lowered herself over him slowly until he was sheathed fully inside her. They groaned in unison. Julia felt the warm waves begin to ripple through her instantly. Her eyes shot to his only to find Seth staring at her in amazement – she hadn't yet moved and already her climax had begun. Her whole body throbbed in anticipation.

Then she felt him shudder beneath her – it was happening to him, too! She forgot to breathe. He held her hips so tight neither could move as they experienced the fiery sensations together. And all the while his gaze held hers, unwavering in its intensity, speaking of things they hadn't yet voiced out loud.

Within seconds she felt the burning heat as his seed shot into her, warming her, filling her. His whole body shook with the strain of trying to remain completely still. Wave after wave flowed through her, centering on the hot place where they were joined and she couldn't help but cry out his name when it all became too much.

As she collapsed against his chest, she felt his racing heart, an echo of her own. All her nerves quivered and still they remained locked together.

Spent, Seth's eyes drifted closed.

"We're both prisoners–," he murmured as he continued to hold her tight, "–happy prisoners. Did I tell you that I love you?"

*

Jamal discreetly approached the auditor who busily pored over a stack of printouts. "Good morning, Mr Lee. Can I have a word?"

Edward Lee glanced up and tugged his wire-rimmed spectacles down his nose. "Certainly, Mr Almose, what can I do for you?"

Jamal pulled up a chair on the opposite side of the desk. "I didn't know what to make of this – these papers appeared on my desk a few days ago. I don't know who put them there, but see this?" He placed a sheet of paper before the auditor and indicated a series of transactions that were highlighted with a pink marker pen. "It looks like someone has been doing a little unauthorized trading. And here," he put forward a second sheet, "and again here," he stuck a third sheet on the desk. "I thought you might want to look into it. It appears someone has been trading in the futures and short term money markets, but the profits have been diverted to a completely different account."

Lee scrutinized the papers, obviously noting the same irregularities that Jamal had seen. "Do you know who owns the account that receives the transfers? – it could be legitimate trading on our client's behalf."

"Yeah, I thought so myself, at first – but the recipient account is situated in the Caymans and appears to be in the name of a shelf company. I haven't been able to find out who actually owns it, as yet, but it all looked a bit odd. Whoever put this on my desk obviously thought the same thing."

"Ahhh," Lee murmured by way of agreement. "I'd better check this thoroughly. Thank you for drawing it to my attention."

Jamal nodded. "Sure – it's my job, isn't it?"

Lee pushed his spectacles up his nose and turned to his computer typing in the Securities and Exchange Commission's URL. Jamal could tell by the eager expression on Lee's face that he took great delight in these kinds of investigations.

Ten

"Here we are," Seth said as he swept her into the formal entry. Setting her overnight bag beside a large earthenware pot, he motioned for Julia to precede him.

Like his office and the boardroom at the bank, his apartment appeared large and airy. At the centre of the massive living room was a glass-ceilinged atrium filled with exotic plants. A miniature waterfall trickled into a tiny Japanese pond, flanked by an array of magnificent bonsai. At the very centre stood a cylindrical tank filled with brightly colored, tropical fish.

Bird, she noted when she stepped closer to the garden, already sat happily on a branch of one of the smaller trees, munching away on sunflower seeds.

"You'll have to watch him with those seeds," she commented with a grin, "I don't think sunflowers will suit the decor."

Seth shrugged. "A man from the nursery tends the garden once a week – he can deal with any stray seeds. Bird looks like he belongs up there."

"Mmmm – I expect we'll never get him to come down. He'll probably be a real pain when it comes time to leave."

Turning sharply, he frowned. "Why would you want to leave?" he threw an arm around her shoulders and drew her close. "I thought we agreed we're together for keeps."

"Yes ... but–"

"But what?" he asked, one eyebrow cocked.

"I – I thought, when you said all that stuff about ... about ..." she looked down at her toes, "–this has all happened so fast. The world seems to be spinning out of control.

"Besides, " she looked up into his golden eyes, "you could change your mind about wanting me."

He swung her around and laughed. "Not possible."

"You might think that now, but we should take a little time and consider things. I'll stay a few days – for now – and we can take it from there."

When his frown deepened and he backed up a step, she reached out a hand. "It's not that I'm doubting your sincerity – or what we feel ..." she squeezed his arm and looked deeply into his eyes, " ... there's some stuff you don't know about my past. And I just don't think we should have any secrets. Deal?"

He stared at her, long and hard, before slowly nodding. "Deal."

When he continued to look at her with a questioning expression, she said, "It's a very long story – I promise to tell you everything soon. Okay?"

"Sounds ominous."

"Not really – just complicated," she reassured.

"I guess I can wait." He figured he knew some of it already. Rick was nothing if not thorough and her attempt to take on a new identity had been, in Rick's words, amateurish – though he'd been unable to find out the precise reason why she'd changed her name and rushed half way around the world.

"Now, let me show you around your new abode," he put his forefinger over her lips before she could protest, "if you decide you don't like it – or it comes time to get a bigger place for the kids, we can always relocate, but for the moment, we'll be safe here."

Kids? He's already thinking about children?

She shook her head in disbelief.

Past the garden, the living area opened out onto a semicircular dining room. All the furniture was made of polished timbers, with cushions and draperies of rich blues and greens. To her amazement, several of her photographs from Irene's exhibition, adorned the side walls alongside what appeared to be prints of Egyptian hieroglyphics.

"What are they?"

"Tomb inscriptions. From the burial chamber of Tuthmosis's vizier and lifelong friend. They hint at the slave princess's story but are too vague to provide us any real answers. They've been in my family for years."

"So from the beginning you've known a lot more than you said." She accused, albeit gently.

Seth responded with a sheepish shrug.

Tinted windows extended along the entire external wall and sloped up half the ceiling to give a spectacular panorama of the city. Several office buildings seemed to float in the sky to the east, and to the north, across the bay, she could see the ships docked at the wharves. The sight nearly took Julia's breath away – she couldn't wait to see the view at night.

"You like?"

"I adore," she whispered, her face aglow with wonder.

"Good. Now come and see the rest. First he took her through a gleaming chef's kitchen full of stainless steel and shiny white tiles. He showed her the pantry, laundry and guest bathroom.

"Three bathrooms?"

"Yep, three."

Down a short hall to the right of the living area, was the empty second bedroom, where Seth had already installed all her painting gear. Its external wall also consisted of windows and she could imagine spending many hours here absorbed in her work. "I'll have some furniture brought up, lights – whatever you need. And if you want, we can turn the guest bathroom into a darkroom."

Though it was on the tip of her tongue to tell him to slow down – that she still wasn't sure, the look of childlike delight that crossed his face as he showed about her his home made her keep her misgivings to herself.

"I still intend to give up the photography."

"If that's what you want – though I have to say your work is very good. It'd be a shame to give it away completely." He turned to her, his expression thoughtful. "And there's room for all the digital equipment. We can upgrade all your stuff, the latest computer and printers."

Julia couldn't help but laugh at his enthusiasm. "Hang on a minute! One thing at a time. First of all, I've never done any of my own color prints, I've always left that part to the labs, So going out and getting all that whiz-bang equipment might be an enormous waste of money. Secondly, at least for now, I really want to concentrate on my painting."

Reaching for her, Seth kissed her so deeply even her toes tingled. When he broke the kiss, he skimmed her cheek with his fingertip, whispering, "Whatever you want, babe, but if change your mind, just say the word.

"C'mon," he said, dragging her back down the hall, "there's more to see." As they passed the entry, he grabbed her suitcase.

On the opposite side of the apartment, down a second short hall stood the main bathroom, all white, with a massive spa in the corner. The glass ceiling made her wonder whether people in the nearby buildings could see Seth when he bathed.

"No – the glass is reflective," he stated as if she'd voiced her concern out loud.

"How'd you know what I was thinking?"

"My love, you think with your face – don't ever offer to partner me at bridge – we'd lose."

She gave him an amicable punch on the shoulder as she stepped past into the hall.

As they entered the main bedroom, Seth dropped the suitcase by the bed. This room, like all the others, was also semi-circular in shape with a glass outer wall that extended halfway up the ceiling. His massive bed, a heavy oregon-based futon about six foot square, sat against the opposite wall, between what Julia assumed were walk-in closets. Again, the furnishings, bedspread, cushions and gossamer thin drapes were made from rich shades of green and blue, although she detected a splash of scarlet here and there.

Opening one of the doors, he showed her a closet more than triple the size of the one in her apartment.

"So," he said turning to watch her face, "what do you think of my humble home?"

"I think there's nothing in the least humble about it."

"Yeah, well, it sort of goes with the territory. The bank owns the place – I just rent it. But it's comfortable and the atrium is very relaxing. Do you think you could be happy here?" His face held an uncertainty she'd never have believed she'd ever see.

In answer, she walked into his arms and held on tight. "I'll be happy wherever we are."

His eyes smoldered in response and she knew she'd done the right thing. His hands smoothed down her back to her buttocks and pulled her close, leaving her in no doubt that her unpacking could wait until much later. But the sound of the doorbell halted whatever Seth might've had in mind. Three times it rang in quick succession.

"Shit – who the hell is that? It couldn't be Rick, he has a security card – besides, he's supervising the clean up team at your apartment," he said as they headed toward the foyer.

"Clean up team?"

"Yeah, I thought you'd want your security bond back. And I'm sure your landlord won't hand it over unless the place is all tidied."

She'd wanted to argue that she'd intended to go back and do it herself tomorrow, but the repeating peal of the bell prevented her.

"Wait behind me," Seth warned, wondering how their visitor got by the security guard downstairs.

When the door swung open, his eyes narrowed. "How'd you get into the elevator unannounced?" he demanded when his cousin's face came into view.

A disheveled Jamal, obviously overcome by drink, staggered one step sideways before breaking into a sloppy smile.

"Nice ta' see you, too, Cuz," he waved his hand at Seth and stumbled into the apartment.

"I asked you a question," Seth said harshly, though his anger seemed to wash over his cousin with little effect.

Jamal spotted Julia standing behind Seth and lunged toward her. "And who might this lovely lady be? Let me introduce myself," he continued, pushing past Seth until he breathed into her face. "Jamal Mikal Omar Almose," he bowed formally before her, nearly losing his balance in the process. He righted himself and grinned. "At your service ma'am."

"Ignore him. The fool is drunk." He grabbed his cousin by the arm and began hauling back toward the front door. "Wait here, babe, I'll just take him down to the lobby and get security to call him a cab. Maybe you can make us a pot of coffee while I'm gone."

Jamal didn't resist when Seth led him to the elevator and pushed the button. "Aw, Cuz, can't I even say hi to the lady? She's a good sort – can I have a turn after you?"

Julia's eyebrows shot up and she could tell by Seth's expression, it'd take very little for him to ram his fist through his cousin's face. "C'mon, Jamal. Let's get you downstairs – and just so you know, Julia's off limits to you, she's going to be my wife very soon."

As the elevator door opened, Jamal swung around and tried to head back toward Julia. "Well congratulations! I'll have to kiss the future bride."

Quick as a shot, Seth twisted his cousin's arm and pulled him backward. He glanced up at Julia, the look on his face begging patience. "Won't be long, babe."

After giving him a smile of understanding, she pushed the door until it was only an inch ajar, then made her way to the kitchen to prepare the coffee.

A couple of minutes later as she poured the coffee grounds into the plunger, she felt a pair of arms circle her waist. "That was quick, there must have been a cab waiting right downstairs."

The arms tightened painfully.

"Seth? What are you doing–?"

When she started to turn, a flash of white danced in her peripheral vision, then a foul-smelling cloth covered her mouth. Her upper arm stung.

A syringe?

She tried to struggle, but the arms about her waist squeezed the breath out of her. From a distance she saw that the hands were large and hairy, the fingers long and bony.

You're not Seth.

Seth!

She wanted to cry out but her mouth didn't seem to work.

How strange.

A buzzing filled her ears. The world around her slowed and the kitchen began to tilt and sway, becoming a column of swirling silver. Darkness flowed over her, smothering her mind. Muffled words echoed through her brain, crazy words, sounds with no meaning.

The buzzing grew louder. In the back of her mind she knew she should be fighting it.

But I'm so tired – perhaps tomorrow.

Something hard slammed into the side of her head – but it seemed so far away, she didn't really feel it.

Eleven

By the time Seth returned to the apartment his anger verged on boiling over. Just as he'd bundled his ridiculous cousin into the cab, the man turned and vomited all over him. No doubt his shoes and jeans were ruined – nothing would get rid of such a stench! Only Jamal could be that repulsive. The cab driver wasn't too happy, at least not until Seth flashed the hundred dollar bill at him.

Entering the apartment, he told himself he'd have to talk to Julia about leaving the door unlocked. Bird squawked loudly and flew straight at him before circling and returning to a higher branch in a wild flutter, feathers raining down.

Seth frowned. The parrot was probably stressed by the strange new habitat, he thought. Or maybe Bird was offended by the disgusting smell – Seth knew he was.

"Hey, babe?" he called in the direction of the kitchen. "I'm just going to take a quick shower – Jamal decided to throw up all over the place. I won't be long."

Less than ten minutes later, he strolled into the kitchen clad only in his bath towel.

"How's that coffee com–"

He stopped dead in his tracks when he saw the broken coffee pot lying on the floor. Coffee grounds were scattered all over and a sickly sweet smell filled the air.

"Julia?" A terrible sense of foreboding flooded his chest. He skirted the glass and quickly checked the pantry, then laundry. *The bathroom – maybe she cut herself.*

"Babe? Are you in here?" The bathroom door crashed against the wall. Empty.

Racing through the apartment, he searched every room, every niche or recess, calling out her name.

When she didn't answer an icy cold sensation gripped his heart, a raw ache that opened up like an old wound.

"JULIA!!!!"

Nothing. Not a sound. His body temperature rose sharply.

She's gone.

Seth grabbed the wall phone and dialed the security guard downstairs. "Peter – did Julia come by with anyone just now?"

"No, Mr Almose, nobody's been past since you went upstairs."

Seth's hand fisted as the fear filled his chest. If they'd taken her, it could already be too late. Adrenalin pumped into his veins, making his heart beat at a feverish pace.

"What about the parking levels? Did she show up on the cameras?"

"Not that I saw – I can get the guys to run the tapes back, if you'd like. What's up, Mr Almose?"

"Julia's gone missing."

"Maybe she just stepped out to get something at the drugstore," Peter offered.

Slamming his fist on the breakfast bar, he growled, "You don't understand – she's been kidnapped, I know it. Get those tapes checked – now! Call me as soon as they've seen it." Slamming the phone down, he instantly picked it up again to dial Rick's number.

"She's gone – they've taken her."

"How do you know?"

Seth wanted to yell with frustration. "I just do! Now get back here. We've got to find her before they hurt her." His heart twisted in his chest – what if they did the same things that were done to the slave girl all those centuries ago? What if they tortured her and raped her. God. He'd never forgive himself if they'd hurt her.

Flying into the bedroom, he grabbed the first clothes he found and dragged them on, then picked up the bedside phone and called security again.

"Have they had a look?" he demanded.

"Mr Almose?"

"Yeah, Pete, what can you tell me?" He held the phone tight, hoping beyond hope that the security guys had noticed something.

"The elevator cameras just show a hand where the occupant pressed the buttons. The camera is positioned above the floor button panel. Whoever used the elevator must have stood flush against the doors."

"Damn." Seth's stomach began to roil. "So you've got nothing?"

"Well ... there could be something on the tape from the parking levels. Perhaps you'd better go down and take a look yourself – just at the very edge of a couple of frames, Joe says he saw two strange men getting into an old sedan. The view is fairly obscure, but he reckons they didn't look like the residents who usually use that particular parking bay."

"I'm on my way." He threw the phone onto the bed without bothering to hang up. As he passed the front hall he grabbed his keys and his cell phone. The front door he left hanging open.

The ride down to the security office seemed to take forever and by the time elevator doors whooshed open, his inner sense of alarm had climbed to screaming point.

"Show me what you've got!"

Joe, the elder of the two attendants, slowly rewound the sequence on the computer, until he got to the frames in question. Pointing at the edge of the grainy gray image that showed only a part of a car obscured by a large Land Rover, he said, "There – you can just see a guy looking around as if checking if anyone's about." He pressed the frame advance several times. "And here, you see? – he's gettin' into the car." Joe kept hitting the advance key, and frame-by-frame the image moved forward. "Now look at this," he tapped on the screen, "another guy comes around and opens the back door, but he doesn't get in. He pushes down the lock button then closes the door again."

Joe spun around and faced Seth with a quizzical expression. "Now why do you think he did that? My guess is he had something in the back seat and he wanted to make sure it stayed there."

When Joe let the file run, Seth saw the car back out of the view of the camera. "Did any other cameras pick up the car? Can you tell the make, or plate number?"

The guard shook his head. "No – either the driver knew the placement of the cameras and how to avoid them, or they parked in another section of the car park and swapped cars. One of our guards is doing a sweep of all the parking levels now."

"But how'd they get through security in the first place? Don't you need a pass?"

Joe and the other guard exchanged a curious look.

"Well, it's like this: residents need a pass, just like the one you have. Some of the merchants on the shopping and restaurant levels have access. And, to cover costs, a small number of day parking spaces are available to the public. There's a separate entrance. They pay fifteen bucks for 3 hours and they're not supposed to have access to the residents' parking levels. We police it ... but ... ?" He shrugged.

Seth could feel his blood begin to boil in his veins. Why hadn't Rick checked this out before giving the all clear?

"My suggestion, Mr Almose, is that you go back to your apartment and call the cops. If your friend has been kidnapped, they're equipped to deal with it."

"Perhaps you're right." Seth dragged a hand across his eyes. He didn't know where to begin searching – maybe the police were his best bet right now.

He stood, knowing Rick probably waited upstairs. "Can you make a few copies of that file? – I expect the police will want to see it – my personal security man, too." At the door to the office, he turned back. "Do you guys have any idea what sort of car that was?"

Each man shook his head. "The only thing I can say is it was probably pretty old," Joe offered with a none-too-reassuring look, "because it had those skinny, push down buttons to lock the doors – most new cars are central locking, or the mechanism's in the armrests. And the taillights were an older style, the kind with chrome rims – most late model vehicles have all plastic fittings. Maybe the cops have an expert who'll know the make and model from the shape of the brake lights and be able to trace the car."

An awful, sinking feeling filled Seth as he went out the door – he sincerely hoped Joe was right.

Twelve

A radio played – a horse race – drowning out the muted voices from the front seat. Air wheezed in through the mesh that covered Julia's face and she didn't try to suppress the groan that rose up her throat as she came fully awake. The gag in her mouth muffled the sound and she had to fight the urge to heave. She could feel a fiery burn where the mesh constantly abraded her cheek and the coarse fabric clung in several places with a warm stickiness. It had obviously broken the skin. Or perhaps the blood came from when they'd hit her. She couldn't recall much, except the gag, a stinging sensation and then a hollow thud, before the hum blessedly carried her into unconsciousness.

Her head ached terribly and she wondered how long she'd been lying facedown on the floor. The hump in the middle forced her forehead against the base of the seat in front, and every bump or turn brought tears to her eyes as the metal ground into her skull. Her hands were tethered painfully beneath her. Her feet were crushed against the door.

She stifled a whimper; she could do nothing until they reached their destination.

Where was Seth? Did he know she was gone? Maybe he followed already.

Please, God, let Seth find me soon.

Although she struggled to stay awake, she couldn't help drifting in and out of consciousness. Lack of air and headache overcame her flagging will, and she dozed again.

When she jerked awake the car had stopped. How far they'd traveled, she had no idea. For long minutes she lay silently awaiting her assailants' next move.

Suddenly, the door by her head sprang open.

Please let it be Seth!

Rough hands dug at her shoulders, pushing her back until she sat on her haunches. The door behind her opened and a second set of hands yanked her backward. She fell, sprawling on her back, completely winded. Unable to breathe she panicked and struggled to draw her own hands up to dislodge the gag, but her captor got there before her, wrenching her hands away before he pulled her upright. She began to heave and choke.

Was this what asthma was like?

Someone took a tight hold of the mesh bag that covered her head, dragging her sideways until she tilted completely off balance. Then a low voice whispered beside her ear, "Calm down and I'll take off the gag. Scream once and it goes back on." He shook the bag so violently her ears rang. "Do you understand?"

Julia shook pitifully as she slowly nodded her head.

Anything to be rid of the gag.

Behind her neck, sharp fingers twisted at the torturous knot. Some hair must have become caught up in the tie and she couldn't help a muted squeal as she felt a large clump come away with the cord as it released. When fingers dug into her mouth and pulled out the wad of saliva-soaked cloth she felt so relieved she wanted to cry.

Drawing in a deep, shuddering breath she forced herself to remain silent and still as her kidnapper removed the cords which bound her ankles. She didn't want to antagonize her captors, vowing to herself that she'd do whatever they wanted if it meant buying enough time to be rescued. Or find a means of escape – whichever came first. At least with her feet free and the gag gone, she'd have a fighting chance.

Still unable to see through the mesh of the bag, she stumbled to one knee when her captor shoved from behind. Fire arced up her leg, stealing the air from her lungs. Tears welled in her eyes but she refused to let them fall; refused to utter a sound. Even with the bag over her head, she promised herself she would maintain her dignity. Right now, it was all she had left.

"Straight ahead," the kidnapper whispered as he gripped her arm in a crushing hold, then lifted her and propelled her another pace forward. "Walk."

Julia obeyed, though each step caused an excruciating pain to shoot up her leg. Her jeans had done little to cushion the fall and her knee throbbed like it did when, at ten, she'd broken her kneecap falling off her bike. She'd never forget that agony. Already her knee was getting hot and tight, and she knew that if she got out of this alive, she'd probably have to cut the jeans from her leg.

"Three stairs," the voice said.

With care, she half-jumped, half-hopped up each step, thankful her captor had hold of her arm because she didn't think she'd have made it otherwise. All of a sudden the atmosphere around her felt cooler and she surmised they must be under a porch or awning.

"Another step."

Julia lifted her uninjured leg and felt for the step.

Once inside, her nose twitched as the overpowering smell of beer – that sickly sweet odor of hops – struck her. Was that where they'd taken her? A bar or tavern? No sounds accompanied the smell, and though she couldn't be sure, her reckoning put the time at late afternoon or early evening. If it was a bar, it attracted little business.

One of her captors maneuvered her onto what felt like a couch. "Stay still and keep quiet," he warned before walking away.

Julia waited and listened intently as the men went into another room. She had no idea whether they could see her or not, but after several minutes of silence, she slowly lifted her arms to hook one thumb under the edge of the mesh bag. Ever so slowly she lifted it until, at last, she could see.

The room where she sat appeared to be an ordinary living room, in an ordinary house, with few furnishings. To her left was a crude bar. Empty bourbon bottles were scattered across it, along with half-filled bottles of beer. Several flies feasted on the remains of a pizza. On a low table before her were more beer bottles and an overflowing ashtray. The floor was littered with bottle caps and sweet wrappers. Obviously, none of the house's occupants knew about keeping house or hygiene.

To her left stood an open doorway that led to a kitchen. As she watched, she saw glimpses of two men; both dressed in black, leaning against one of the cabinets. One turned her way and her breath caught.

Dropping the bag instantly, she prayed he hadn't seen her looking. After several long seconds, when neither man returned, she assumed he hadn't.

So, she thought with a mixture of anger and dismay – Gerry *was* in on it. She should have known. His aggressive behavior in recent weeks and her innate feelings of unease in his presence should have warned her long ago. *Easy in hindsight.* The other man, she hadn't really seen, but she could guess his identity. Tobias probably.

Just as she was about to hazard lifting the bag again, a car pulled up outside. *Seth?* – her heart begged. *Please let it be Seth!*

A moment later she heard the front door open and close.

"Shit!" the new man said as he crossed the room with heavy steps. "Are you two mad? You left her here by herself – she could have run away dammit!"

"Not likely–," Gerry replied with his usual silkiness, "–she fell on the way in and banged her leg up good. She wouldn't make it to the front gate."

Julia knew he was right. A sense of desolation flooded her chest.

"Still, you should be watching her. There are houses all around us, all she'd have to do is get to a neighbor's and we'd be done for. So stay alert you fools and keep your mind on the job at hand."

As she listened, she realized that the voice of the third man sounded vaguely familiar. She'd heard it only recently, of that she was absolutely certain, but where, she couldn't quite recall.

"So, how'd it go at your end?" – this from the other kidnapper, the one Julia suspected was Tobias.

"Like a charm. The auditor took the bait with glee."

"And Seth?"

"He had no idea it was a diversion, whether he's worked it out yet, is anyone's guess. But it's of no consequence – it's now just a matter of time." He laughed out loud then said with obvious self-satisfaction, "You wouldn't believe it – I purposely threw up all over him – a talent I learnt at summer camp. You should've seen the horrified look on his face – it was classic. How I'm going to relish his downfall."

Julia ignored the men's laughter as another piece of the puzzle clicked into place. That's where she'd heard the voice – Seth's cousin, Jamal. For the first time something made sense. From what she'd deduced from all her dreams and the stories Seth told her about his ancestors, the ultimate reason for the curse was power. Originally, it seemed to be a power struggle between Tuthmosis and the Retennu princes. Was Jamal attempting to wrest power from Seth? – did he want to take Seth's position at the bank?

Before that scenario had a chance to take hold another chilling thought occurred to her. In not only her dreams, but also several of Seth's stories, the girl endured more than just kidnapping. Dear God, did they intend the same for her? Would they whip her or rape her? Even murder her? An uncontrollable shaking took hold of her body as the full magnitude of her plight sank in. She was crippled, had no weapons and no leverage to bargain with. And whatever they planned for Seth, she'd be no help to him at all unless she could devise a means to warn him.

Her head shot up as the front door clicked open. Her heart in her throat, Julia waited and prayed that this time Seth had come to rescue her. The door closed quietly, almost without a sound. Her pulse began to race. Surely it was Seth, being stealthy.

"Oh, so you made it," Gerry stated to the newcomer in a caustic tone.

Julia ached to cry out with disappointment.

"Of course – I didn't want to miss all the fireworks."

It shocked Julia to hear the accented female voice.

"I see we have our hostage all parceled up. When do we start the final phase?" the woman continued.

"This time tomorrow the cops should be dragging him off to jail, suspected of illegal share trading and fraud."

To Julia's mind, Gerry sounded almost gleeful.

"Sounds perfect."

"Yes indeed."

Julia strained to hear as their voices became more subdued. She heard the rasp of material, and, if she wasn't mistaken, the sound of two people kissing – passionately.

"And later tonight," Gerry's continued in a whisper, "Jamal will go back to the bank and move the rest of what's rightfully ours. He'll be CEO before week's end, I should think. Then, once we have control, the sky'll be the limit."

Julia's hands fisted. *Just wait until Seth arrives!*

*

Seth's cell phone was beeping loudly when he returned to the apartment.

"Almose." He ground the word in low tones, unable to control the feeling of frustration that welled inside his chest.

"Good afternoon, Seth, Edward here."

"Hello Edward, look, I don't mean to be rude, but if this isn't urgent can I call you back? I'm in the middle of a crisis – it appears that someone has kidnapped my fiancée."

"Oh ... Ah ... well that could make what I have to tell you even more important, Seth."

Seth clenched his fists and wondered what else might be in store. "Okay, Edward, but make it quick."

"Well, it has been drawn to my attention that a member of the executive staff has been engaging in some unauthorized, and none-too-legal, money market trading using clients funds."

Hell! That's all the bank needs, Seth thought with a frown. "Are you certain?"

"No mistake."

"Still it can wait ... Julia is more important."

"Perhaps, but this might not be a coincidence."

Seth reeled for a moment. But Edward could be right. And it might mean they can flush out the kidnapper.

"Any idea who is behind it – who has been doing the trading?"

There was a long pause at the other end of the line, and the hair at Seth's nape began to prickle.

"Well, that's just it. I tracked all the transactions, twice to be sure ... and ... I hate to say it, my friend, but all the evidence points to you."

"*What!*" Seth didn't mean to yell but he couldn't help himself. It was the exact idea he'd presented to the board only days ago – they'd automatically assume he was responsible.

"Look, Seth, I've known you long enough to know this is not your style – that it's probably a set up. But you must understand, I'm bound by law in this kind of situation, I must report this to the authorities."

With a tired sigh, Seth stared skyward as if he'd somehow be able to call on divine inspiration. "Yeah, Edward, I know, and I wouldn't ask you to compromise your position for me–," suddenly, an idea struck him, "–but ... is it possible to wait a day or two before you make an official report?"

"I guess so, but what will that achieve?"

"I'm not sure, but I think I know who might be behind this. Can you tell me how you found out about it?"

"An anomaly was detected by a member of the executive staff and reported to me."

"What kind of anomaly?"

"Briefly, some illegal transactions were made using borrowed client funds, then the profits were diverted into an offshore account in the name of a shelf-company. After some digging, I found that the company belonged to you."

"But I don't own any offshore companies or accounts."

"I know. That's why I wanted to speak to you first – just to be certain you hadn't opened any since we went over your personal accounts, late last year."

"I haven't."

"That leaves me in a quandary, though. I'm bound by law to report this to the Securities and Exchange Commission. The bank accounts are definitely in your name, so if you didn't open them, someone else did. Someone who could make it appear legitimate."

"And for the express purpose of implicating me – who made the report?"

Another long pause. "I shouldn't really divulge that information, Seth, but if it helps you straighten this out, I suppose it won't hurt – it was your cousin, Jamal."

Seth felt his blood heat. It all suddenly fit ... the drunken visit ... Julia's disappearance ... now this. Why hadn't he seen it coming? Time and again Jamal had deliberately made a point of baiting him since he'd come to Boston. Seth had continually tried to deny his suspicions where his cousin was concerned, always putting it down to familial rivalry. But now he knew. It had to be the curse.

"How much time can you give me without getting yourself into trouble, Edward?"

"I could probably hold off until Monday, I should check all the reports and printouts again. Will that be enough time?"

"It'll have to be. Listen, can you fax over everything you've got so far, so I can take a look? And can you also get the offshore banks involved to send copies of all the paperwork relating to the bank accounts. Also anything you can get on the shelf company. It might be wise to check if there are other incidents. Backtrack a little, see if you can detect any other unusual transactions – we can't afford for any of the bank's clients to be affected."

"Will do. Let me know if there's anything else I can do to help," Edward said with the kind of warmth that came from long-standing friendship.

"Yeah, I will. I'll talk to you later – and thanks."

Seth shut off the phone, lowered himself onto the couch and tried to rub the weariness from his eyes.

He was just about to dial 911 when Rick burst into the apartment.

"What happened?" demanded the former detective as he strode across the room.

Seth motioned toward the kitchen, "In here," he said before briefly explaining the course of events since they'd parted earlier in the day.

The rich aroma of ground coffee filled the air.

"What do you think?" Seth asked after Rick had examined the mess on the floor.

Tight concern etched Rick's features. "Well, I'd say they surprised her from behind. There's no blood that I can see, which is a positive." He circled around the glass and squatted down to look under the cupboards and fridge. Small bits of glass littered the floor along with the coffee, but he could see little else. "Any idea who might have done this?"

"Yeah, I'm betting it's one of Jamal's friends. He staggered in here just before Julia disappeared, seemingly drunk, but now I wonder if it wasn't an act. At some point, either when I was taking him down to the cab, or while I showered–," he grimaced as he recalled the way Jamal threw up all over his legs and feet, "–whoever did this made their move. When I came back into the kitchen I found it like this. Time wise, the whole episode could only have taken ten, maybe fifteen, minutes.

"I wasn't suspicious of Jamal at first, but Edward, the bank's auditor, called a minute ago – it seems Jamal handed him some transaction printouts that implicate me in illegal money-market trading.

"So now I'm more than suspicious."

Rick carefully studied the room one more time, before going to check the lock on the front door. Unless you were looking for it, you wouldn't notice – but a length of clear tape lay discarded in the hallway just outside the door. Very carefully, he picked it up and examined it.

"You got a small bag?" he asked Seth as he waved the tape in front of his eyes.

"What is it?"

"Tape – my guess is your cousin stuck this over the lock to prevent the door shutting properly. You'd better call the police. I'll head across to Jamal's place and see if I can't find anything there."

"Hang on a moment," Seth said as he went into his study. When he emerged he held a set of keys. "These are the spare keys to Jamal's apartment. He doesn't know I have copies. If he's not there, you have the bank's 'permission' to inspect the premises."

Rick smiled his agreement.

"If you find anything at all, call me."

With a nod, Rick left Seth to call the police.

*

It seemed to take hours. The first contingent of police came and after making a cursory inspection of the kitchen and recording all the details of Seth's story, went again – only to be replaced by technicians who searched for fingerprints and took samples from the spilled coffee and glass on the floor. They photographed the room from every angle.

While they worked Seth checked his watch constantly and racked his brain for ideas as to Julia's whereabouts. He replayed every conversation he'd had with his cousin over the past few weeks hoping the fool had said or done something that might provide even the smallest clue. If this was the curse at work, time was of the essence and he worried that as each moment passed, she'd slip further and further away. Pacing the room like a caged tiger, he willed them to hurry and finish so he could call Rick for a report.

The detective-in-charge, a balding man with a ruddy face and keen eyes named Daryl Kirkman, returned soon after the technicians left.

"Have you thought of anything else, Mr Almose?" Kirkman asked as he crossed the threshold.

Seth shook his head.

"And there's been no ransom call?"

Again Seth shook his head.

The fax machine clicked on and a sheet of paper began to emerge. Seth went over and glanced at it. It was the first of the pages that Edward had promised to forward.

"Something important?" Kirkman asked as he edged closer.

Seth stepped casually between Kirkman and the machine and looked him in the eye. "Just bank business," he answered in a non-committal tone. He hadn't told the police about the attempt to frame him and didn't intend to, at least not until he knew more.

"Is it possible that Ms Morrow's disappearance is related to your business dealings, Mr Almose?"

Tilting his head, Seth pretended to consider the idea. "I don't think it's likely," he said after a moment. "Julia has had no involvement with my business at all."

"What if a business rival is attempting to get at you through her?"

Seth looked over at one of her photographs. He wished he could tell Kirkman the truth – but he really couldn't say what the truth was, precisely. He only had the lessons of history to go on, and Kirkman's no-nonsense manner strongly suggested he wouldn't buy into any of it.

"I doubt it – despite what people hear, most of us bankers are honest men. I take pride in maintaining a reputation for integrity, and

I can almost guarantee that none of my business dealings would be in any way responsible for Julia being kidnapped."

Kirkman studied Seth's face for several beats. "Ms Morrow might have left of her own volition, Mr Almose. Have you considered that? Are you certain that you didn't have a disagreement of some kind?"

The glare Seth shot at the detective should have burned the flesh from the man's bones.

"Well," Kirkman sniffed, then walked the length of the living area to admire the spectacular view. "What we'll need to do is tap the phone, in case the perpetrator decides to call with ransom demands. We're analyzing the video files at the moment, and should know if they hold any worthwhile leads within an hour or two.

"Needless to say, Mr Almose, we'd like you to remain in the apartment—"

"But what if–?"

Kirkman held up a hand to stay any argument. "We're very good at what we do, Mr Almose. Don't get in our way. The best thing you can do for Ms Morrow is be here for her when she returns."

Any resistance Seth might have thrown up was squashed the instant Rick came through the door.

"Hello, Daryl," he greeted Kirkman with raised brows, "are you on this?"

"Yeah, buddy. What're you doing here?"

Kirkman turned to Seth. "You didn't say anything about a private investigator working on this."

"That's because I'm his full-time security man," Rick put in. "Don't worry, I'll give you anything I get, but I'll expect the same from you."

Kirkman's brow creased, but he didn't respond.

Rick looked at Seth and grinned. "Kirkman and I worked together a few years back while I was still on the force. You can trust him."

It was Kirkman's turn to grin. "I reckon you already know you can trust Rick.

"I'll keep you to that promise, Rick," Kirkman warned his old friend. "If this *is* a kidnapping, the lady's life could be at stake, so any information you get will be passed on immediately so we can bring in the FBI. Right?"

"You got it." Rick glanced across at Seth, saying without words that he needed to speak to him about the errand he'd just returned from.

Seth replied with an almost imperceptible nod before asking Kirkman if he could have the kitchen cleaned.

"Yeah, go ahead, we've got all we need." He checked his watch. "I'll head back to base and see whether they've got any information on the car. Our IT people should be here to set up soon." He pulled out his iPhone and raised his eyes expectantly. "I'd better get your number as well, Rick. If I can't get Mr Almose, I'll contact you."

After giving Kirkman the number, Rick escorted him to the door. The two men stood talking for several minutes before Rick shut the door and returned to the living room.

"What was that all about?" Seth asked.

"I just told him that I had a lead that I planned on chasing down. I assured him it was only a hunch, but I'd let him know if it became solid. And I will," he gave Seth a hard stare. "I wasn't joking when I said you can trust him. He's the best, and the only reason I didn't tell him about our suspicions, was the business with Edward at the bank. We don't want your assets frozen unnecessarily, and that's what'll probably happen if SEC starts investigating. I reckon that's what the bastard is after – tie you up in a legal and financial straightjacket. If Edward can get to the bottom of it quickly, we can avoid all that and stop the bastard before he really gets started."

"He's already started – he's taken Julia." Seth spat the words.

Rick's jaw tightened before he said, "We'll get her back."

"We'd better," Seth replied in a low voice. "What did you find at Jamal's place?"

Rick crossed the room and threw himself onto a dining chair. He emptied his pockets, tossing scraps of paper, dockets and credit card receipts onto the table.

"I went over the place with a fine-toothed comb – apart from the furniture, and a pile of bedding that lay in the laundry, everything seemed remarkably clean – like he didn't plan on returning to the place anytime soon. I did, however, find a few items that could help us. They were in the recycling bin."

"Oh?" He had a lot of trouble imagining Rick digging through the trash.

"Yeah. This," he held up what appeared to be an invoice. In fact, it was an account dated more than three months earlier, from an international business agent billing him for search fees.

"Now why would Jamal need to search out prospective international companies?" Seth murmured to himself.

He picked up another scrap, a rent receipt from a realtor in Brockton. His brow knitted in speculation, he glanced up at Rick. "Have you got an address?"

"I'm waiting to hear from a contact."

"I'd say my cousin has just about confirmed our suspicions."

"Looks like." Rick reached across and unfolded several other pieces of paper. "This one's interesting ... " he held up a torn sheet, " ... from an IT consultant in Atlanta. It's an emailed memo that says: *need superuser password – root privilege – alter server's internal clock/return when done.*

"I spoke to Avery Singh, the bank's IT tech and he says the superuser password–"

"–is my high security password that allows me to tap into the main server's administration level. That and the SecureID token. Technically, I'm the only one who knows that password, and I change it regularly. How would Jamal have gotten hold of it?"

"Do you keep a copy anywhere?"

"Apart from the office safe – only in my personal safety deposit box at the bank, and that's where I left the token before going out of town ... hang on," his eyes narrowed as the penny dropped. "Of course!" He thumped his thigh with his fist. "How damned stupid – I gave Jamal power of attorney when I went overseas a few months ago. I remember telling him he should memorize the number just in case I had an accident. He laughed the suggestion off and said that if he needed to use the power of attorney, he'd have Carolynne get the number from the safe. Otherwise, it 'wasn't worth taxing his brain' to memorize it, he said.

"When I got back, Carolynne said that Jamal hadn't needed to execute any formal contracts and hadn't asked for the number, or the papers." He turned to stare out the window at the darkening sky, the sense of foreboding now multiplying itself by the minute. "I didn't think anymore about it."

"I'd say cousin Jamal memorized that number," Rick scowled. "We'd better check if the box has been opened."

Seth went to the phone, dialed Edward's direct line and gave him the information. Edward promised to verify activity on the safety deposit box, and check the main computer's administration log for the dates surrounding the transactions to see if any administrative changes could be detected.

"Can you also find out from security if Jamal has been working odd hours over the past couple of months, and if so, when. If he has been tampering with the computer ... the times should marry up."

"Sure thing, Seth – I'll get back to you if I find even the smallest anomaly. By the way, if you can sign and fax back that form I sent a while ago, I'll have copies of those bank account registrations by this time tomorrow – that should tell us who actually opened them."

"I expect we already know the answer to that one," Seth muttered through clenched teeth.

"Perhaps," Edward agreed. "But still, I'd like to have everything in order before I put it before the SEC."

"Okay Ed, let me know the minute you have anything definite."

"Will do."

As soon as he hung up, Seth headed for the fax machine – the faster he got those forms back, the faster he'd have a clear-cut answer on Jamal's involvement.

*

The pounding in her head had gotten worse. If only she could allow herself some sleep, but she knew that she needed to keep her wits about her and not be caught unawares.

Shortly after the woman arrived, Gerry and Tobias took themselves off to buy food. Jamal had gone somewhere too, but she had no idea where.

If ever there was an opportunity to escape ...

Julia knew the woman remained in the room; her expensive French perfume wafted about in occasional bursts, contrasting with the smell of stale beer and pizza.

"You won't get away with this, you know," Julia said, hoping to get the woman to talk so she could work out exactly where the woman was in relation to the front door.

"Oh?" the woman sounded unconcerned. "Whatever makes you think that?"

Julia turned her head in the direction of the woman's voice, which came from somewhere, Julia guessed, near the kitchen doorway. Her quick peek earlier told her that a barstool sat over by the archway that led to the kitchen. The woman was probably just sitting there, watching her. Julia could hear her breathing.

It reminded Julia of the sick, hollow feeling she had when she realized she was being spied upon by the stalker. Nausea rose to burn the back of her throat but she tamped it down, knowing she couldn't afford to indulge her fears now.

If her estimation was correct, the woman sat between her and the only escape route – and the woman didn't have the added impediment of being half crippled and blind.

There must be a way to get her to leave the room.

"Seth is smarter than you think – he'll work it out before you get too much further, if he hasn't already," Julia said – she needed to keep the woman talking so she'd know if she moved.

The woman laughed. "If Seth was so smart he would have married me years ago and could've avoided all this."

Julia heard the woman move closer, then, suddenly, the mesh bag flew from her head. Her forehead began to sting and she knew her grazed skin had opened up again when a warm trickle began slowly tracking down the side of her face.

"What he sees in you, I really don't know," she snarled as she stepped back, tossing the bag on the couch alongside Julia. "A mousy little girl-next-door type, aren't you?"

The instant her eyes adjusted to the bright light, Julia was surprised to find her adversary wasn't the woman she'd expected. In fact, she had never laid eyes on her. She'd assumed that the woman would be the dark-haired one with the hard features, who'd hung upon Seth's arm at the showing a few weeks ago.

Was it only a few weeks? – it seemed as if years had passed since that first fateful meeting with Seth. So much had happened – her life bore no resemblance to the one she lived then. Her face probably bore no resemblance to that girl either – her lips felt bruised and parched, and the side of her head swollen and bloody from where the bag grazed her cheek.

After blinking a couple of times, Julia focused on the woman's face and realized she could have passed as a double for one of the characters of her dreams. Her hair and coloring were different, but the essential features were very like the cruel woman who'd flashed into her mind when she remembered the torture.

"What? No answer to that one?" The woman crossed her arms and loomed over Julia with a sneer, her exotic beauty diminished by the obvious ugliness of her thoughts.

With a shake of her head, Julia quelled the desire to kick out at her – if she wanted to gain an advantage, she'd have to choose her moment well.

"You really don't know who I am, do you?" the woman asked, though she didn't wait for an answer. "I'm Celine Steele – my uncle and Seth's father were business associates. Seth and I have been friends since childhood."

Julia raised an eyebrow – the woman before her and the Seth she knew didn't seem in the least compatible as friends, or anything else.

"Yes, so you needn't look surprised. Seth and I should be married now, but he broke off our relationship just before his father sent him to this godforsaken city to run the bank. Needless to say, I knew Seth didn't want to leave me – he just felt compelled to please his father, who, for some reason known only to himself, didn't want our relationship to continue."

Celine began pacing in front of Julia, but wasn't really paying attention to her at all.

Julia willed Celine to move further away from the front door; this may be the chance she'd been waiting for.

"I came here a few months ago. I knew he hadn't meant to break it off. But just as I'd begun to get through to him, you turned up with your fancy painting and all those seductive looks," she spun about and glared at Julia in the same instant Julia had planned to spring off the couch and bolt for the door. "I saw you that night, acting so coy and innocent."

"You were there?"

"Yes I was. I took a job as a waitress for the evening. As soon as I saw you I knew you were trouble. The real shrinking violet, you were. And ever the gentleman, Seth wouldn't have been able to resist that waif-like show you put on. You orchestrated it all didn't you – the painting, the invitation to the show."

"What invitation?" Julia knew nothing about any invitations. "Irene and Gerry were responsible for the guest list."

Celine waved the idea away. "I'm not stupid. You deliberately painted the picture knowing it would attract his attention. It wouldn't have taken much digging to learn that Seth is obsessed by Tuthmosis. Actually, I wish I'd thought of it – it would have saved a great deal of effort on my part. Still, he'll be out of your life soon enough – and you'll be well and truly out of his."

She said those last words with a finality that sent a chill all the way down to Julia's toes. Surely this woman wasn't capable of murder?

"You should have paid heed to the warning."

Julia almost flinched ... the voice on the answer machine.

The front door flew open. "Shit, Celine – why'd you take off the hood? She couldn't identify us before – now she can! Are you out of your mind?" Gerry marched across the room and picked up the bag.

"Please, I promise to keep my mouth shut – just don't put it on again," Julia begged.

He stopped; the glare he cast her suggested things she didn't want to think about.

"Not so *high and mighty* now, eh, Julia? Not too good to be nice to me now – funny how circumstances can change things." He leaned over her, breathing onto her face, his expression a mask of self-righteous anger. "No *rain checks*?"

He gripped her jaw and jerked her chin upward so she had to shut her eyes to escape his hateful glare.

"No '*maybe next time, Gerry*'? What a shame – poor, sweet untouchable Julia – well, you can't ignore me this time, can you?" He released her with a sudden shove that sent her reeling against the back of the couch.

Shaking her head from side to side, Julia knew she couldn't deny what he said. "Please, I'll do whatever you want ..."

He bent forward and patted her cheek again, a feral smile exposing a row of too even, too white, teeth. "Now that might be interesting," he leaned closer until his mouth brushed her ear, and he let one finger weave a path down the front of her chest, between her breasts, and lower. Taunting her. As he straightened, he grinned with satisfaction – and Julia knew she couldn't hide the fear from her eyes.

"Perhaps a little later – when we can be alone, eh? I can think of a lot of *'whatevers'* we can do together." He patted her cheek, harder this time, before glaring down at her like she was merely dirt beneath his feet. "Please me, and who knows how all this'll turn out."

She stifled the urge to gag.

The front door opened and Tobias stepped into the room. "Jeeesuss! Now she can indentify us all!"

"It's okay," Celine soothed, "she's promised to be good, haven't you, Julia?" Her sadistic sneer spoke volumes and Julia began to pray in earnest. If she was ever going to make it out of this alive, she'd better come up with an escape plan and quick.

"Here," Tobias said, handing a McDonald's sack to each of her captors.

He glanced down at Julia and instantly an image flashed into her mind. She was looking out her bathroom window two years ago. At those eyes! They were a different color – dark blue instead of a washed-out green. With lighter, longer hair, a clean-shaven chin and those eyes she saw the face of her stalker looking back at her.

A moment of recognition passed between them before his mouth formed a knowing smirk. Adrenalin flooded her veins and her gut became a pit of ice, yet she couldn't even gasp.

"Don't worry, Jules–" his face almost beamed with malicious pride, "–I've got something for you, too."

His eyes seemed to gleam with unspoken promises as he slowly smoothed his free hand over his groin to outline his genitals. He dropped the paper bag onto her lap and sniggered. "Shouldn't be too difficult, even with your hands tied." He raised one slash of a brow and she understood he didn't mean the food.

That gesture sparked other memories – not only of when she'd first seen him masturbating outside her window. Another memory filled her mind ... a darker skinned man with a goatee beard, who'd had the same look in his savage gray eyes ... a man from eons ago, who'd stolen her life and crushed it even as he took his pleasure.

Heart pounding, she swayed where she sat as he turned away and sauntered into the kitchen. She couldn't believe he was here. He'd found her. Her stomach sank until she thought she might faint. How stupid. And naïve. She thought she'd escaped him merely by changing her name and moving overseas.

Oh God. How long has he been watching me this time?

She fought the hysteria forming in her chest. In that instant all her recent dreams transformed into clear remembrances of the life she was now certain she'd once lived. Seth had been right – she was that girl. And if he didn't rescue her soon it might be too late. Again.

Tears began to well in her eyes, but she stifled them. She couldn't afford to give in to self-pity.

Anger and fear made her want to throw the food at his retreating back, but she knew she'd need her strength if she hoped to make her escape. She peered into the bag, half expecting to find a nest of spiders lurking inside. When she saw the burger and fries, she almost whimpered out loud. With only a minimum of struggle, she managed to extricate the carton of fries.

"And after dinner," Gerry said with a smirk, "we'll put you to bed – tied, of course"

Not while I breathe!

*

While Rick followed up on some of the receipts he'd discovered at Jamal's house, Seth went over the reports from Edward and waited for the phone to ring.

The police had installed their phone-tapping device some hours before, and a member of their technology unit sat on Seth's favorite armchair, drinking his coffee, ready to do whatever he needed to do if the kidnappers made contact.

"Do you think they might still ring tonight?" Seth asked the man, making conversation.

With a shrug, the policeman leaned forward and checked his equipment again. "Beats me – no rhyme or reason when it's a kidnapping."

"You've worked on a few?"

"Some. Not one has ever been the same." He looked up at Seth and gave him a compassionate smile. "My advice would be to get some shut-eye, Mr Almose. If they ring tonight, I'll get you straight away – and if they don't, tomorrow's probably going to be a very long one. Best get some rest."

Seth had to admit he was fatigued, but he felt too wound up to sleep. "I might crash out on the couch," he suggested as a compromise, "that way I can be close if they do call."

Again the policeman shrugged. "Suit yourself."

"Feel free to help yourself to anything in the fridge," Seth said as he crossed the room.

Pulling the tie from his ponytail, Seth threaded his fingers into his hair. What he wouldn't give if it were Julia's fingers. Only last night, she'd tugged his hair to bring him closer for her kiss.

It seemed so very long ago.

He laid back and allowed his eyes to close, wondering for the umpteenth time if Julia was still okay. If they'd hurt her, at all, they'd pay with their lives – he'd kill them with his bare hands if he had to. Though he'd never harbored such violent thoughts before, it felt satisfying to play with the idea of vengeance. As sleep took him, he wondered what his ancestor would have done in his place…?

Thirteen

Rick's gentle nudge sent Seth upright in an instant. He blinked several times to orient himself, then, as he realized where he lay, he slumped back onto the cushion.

"What is it?" he asked as he rubbed the sleep from his eyes.

Bending close to Seth's ear, Rick whispered, "I think I've found her."

Seth's head whipped around.

"Shhhh." Rick urged. "Our cop friend is snoozing, and I'd like to keep him out of the loop, for now. I'm going to the kitchen. Follow in a minute or two and I'll tell you what I discovered."

With casual grace for such a big man, Rick straightened and sauntered silently across the room.

Seth glanced over to where the police technician snored quietly. Unable to contain himself beyond the barest minute, he eased himself off the couch and crept to the kitchen.

"What can you tell me?" he asked when Rick looked up.

"I found the house he rented a couple of months ago – it's about half an hour away from here just south of Brockton. I managed to get a look inside, and I'm pretty sure I saw Jamal and that dude from the exhibition where you bought Julia's painting, talking in the front room."

"Gerry van der Gelder?"

"Yep, that's him. Your old flame, Celine, was there, too."

"Celine?" Seth groaned and shook his head at his own stupidity. How obvious it all seemed in hindsight. He knew Celine had never forgiven him for breaking their relationship. She'd turned up on his doorstep several months ago and tried to seduce him. More than once. In the end he'd been almost cruel when she wouldn't take no for an answer.

"Yep, she walked in from the back of the house just as I was about to return to my car. When she spoke, she appeared to be talking to someone – but I couldn't see the other person. My guess is Julia."

Seth's heart rate soared. "Let's go then."

Rick's hand shot out to stay Seth's movement. "Wait. We need to have a plan. We don't know whether they're armed or not. Nor do we know if there are any others."

"Perhaps, but we have the element of surprise. They have no idea we know where they are. At this time of night, some of them will surely be asleep. If we can sneak in, we might be able to get her out without too much hassle."

The look on Rick's face was telling. "First we need some fire power, just in case. We also need to get out of here without being seen – Kirkman will undoubtedly veto any action on our part."

"Then we can think about how we're going to get Julia out – if, indeed, she's there."

"She's there all right, I can feel it," Seth stated with certainty. "We'll have to take our chances as far as weapons go – I don't own a gun and I don't want to go in shooting, anyway. It would only put Julia in more danger."

Rick's eyebrows rose, but a second later he smiled. "You're probably right." He ducked his head around the corner and checked that the technician still slept. "He hasn't moved," he tilted his head toward the technician, "we should be able to get past him if we're quiet and quick. You go first," he handed Seth the address and his car keys, "and I'll meet you at the car in a few minutes. If I'm not there in five, assume the tech. woke and I had trouble getting away."

With a nod, Seth left the room and edged past the sofa where the technician still snored. Once past, he veered around the indoor garden and slipped through the front door to the elevator.

The time seemed to drag while he waited for Rick to appear.

"I'll drive," Rick gesticulated to the passenger seat as he yanked the driver's side door open. "I have a feeling you're on the edge – besides, I already know the way.

With a thunderous scowl, Seth climbed out of the driver's seat and headed around to the passenger side.

They'd been flying down the highway for a while when Rick said, "I think Kirkman's following us."

Fighting the urge to turn in his seat, Seth covertly studied the reflection in the side mirror. He couldn't see anything.

"About a quarter mile back – unmarked cop car," Rick added, his eyes darting between the rearview mirror and the road ahead.

"Are you sure?"

"Fairly sure." Rick checked his side mirror with a casual movement of his eyes. "No matter. He might have been able to hold us at the apartment, but not now." As they approached Pleasant Street, he flicked on the indicator. "Better to have him on our side if it comes down to a fight."

Two turns later, Rick shut off the headlights before easing around the corner and pulling over. "It's the single storey past the second street light," he said pointing down the tree-lined street.

"I see it," Seth said as he felt the adrenalin rush into is system. "What are we going t—" The tap on his window startled him for a second, until he recognized Kirkman's craggy face. Seth pressed the button to lower the glass.

"So," Kirkman grinned as he thrust his head through the window, "got any leads you'd like to share, Rick?"

"Hop in the back, buddy," Rick replied, returning Kirkman's grin. He waited until Kirkman closed the door. "I found a rental slip amongst the papers at Seth's cousin's."

"What has Seth's cousin got to do with this?" Kirkman demanded.

"A lot. It seems wants to get Seth out of the way so he can take over as CEO at the bank – trying to frame him for embezzlement and insider trading. I suspect he kidnapped Julia to distract Seth from his other activities."

Kirkman stuck his head between the two passenger seats, and from the look on his face, Seth assumed the man was pretty peeved.

"Why the hell didn't you tell me any of this before?" Kirkman scowled. "You could have saved me a lot of legwork, *buddy*!"

Rick merely smiled. "I couldn't confirm any of it – and you would have charged in, guns blazing."

"Horseshit!" The windows were beginning to fog with all the heated discussion. "Tell me exactly what you've got."

"They're holed up in that house just past the second street light. Jamal, and a guy called Gerry van der Gelder—"

"The guy who works for Ms Morrow's agent?"

"That's the one. I saw both, and Seth's former girlfriend, Celine, when I checked the place out earlier tonight. I'm not sure if Julia is there – I didn't see her. We were going to sneak up and take a closer look."

The back seat squeaked as Kirkman sat back. "And when were you intending to let me in on all this information?"

Rick turned to face his former colleague. "When I was certain of my facts – same as you would've done."

Until now, Seth had remained silent, but he was getting a little sick of the muscle flexing going on between Rick and Kirkman. "Look, can you two finish your pissing contest at a later date? If Julia's in that house, and my gut says she is, we should be thinking about how to get her out!"

Kirkman and Rick glared at each other for another moment, before each man broke into a smile.

"You're right," Rick admitted, turning back to watch the house. "What do you reckon, Daryl? How d'you want to approach the place?"

"Hang here a minute." Opening the door, Kirkman slid out of the car and trotted across the street so he could take a better look at the house. By the time Seth and Rick had climbed out of the car, Kirkman returned. "Rick, you take the left side – go in through the yard next door. I'll slip in through the other side."

Seth threw out an arm to stop Kirkman as he headed out. "There's no way I'm going to stand here and wait."

Turning back, Kirkman raised one eyebrow and glanced over at Rick.

"It's his lady – what would you do in the circumstances?" Rick said with a shrug.

"Okay, stay behind Rick and keep as quiet as you can. If there's trouble, keep your head down. No heroics – either of you. Besides, it could all be perfectly innocent in there."

Seth snorted.

"You know I should be calling for back-up, Rick. Don't make me regret that I haven't yet."

"Don't worry, bud, Seth's no fool and I haven't forgotten my training." He waved his cell phone at Kirkman. "I'll signal when we're in a good position."

"Okay."

With that, Kirkman again crossed the street and using the trees as cover, began making his way past the house in question.

Rick led Seth along a similar course on the nearside until he reached the neighboring yard. With deliberate slowness, Rick pushed the gate open and crept up the path. After a quick check on Kirkman's progress, Seth followed Rick's lead and drew up beside him where a large bush sheltered them both.

"Lucky there's no dog," Rick whispered. "I'm going to jump the fence and go around the back. Wait a few seconds then try for a spot near the big window out front. If you can get a look inside without anyone catching sight of you, even better. Otherwise, wait until you get a signal from me or Kirkman."

Seth nodded.

With an agile leap, Rick disappeared into the blackness down the side of the house.

Breathing deeply, Seth tried to still his nerves. Julia was close by – he could feel her presence, just like that first time when he'd been drawn to her at the museum, the day she'd come back to secretly see Tuthmosis. He'd sensed her then, though he didn't yet fully understand how or why. He'd stood in the shadows and simply observed her, a feeling of connection flowing through his very marrow. Prescience, he'd thought only a three weeks later when she'd turned out to be the artist of his painting.

And now, that connectedness filled him a hundredfold – which was, in itself, reassuring. It meant she was almost certainly alive.

"You'd better not have hurt her, cousin," he growled inwardly, knowing he wouldn't be responsible for his own actions if Jamal, or that scum, van der Gelder, had so much as laid a finger on her. Sweat broke out on his brow as he recalled Julia's description of the rape and murder of the young princess. If either man had harmed her in any way – if either had ... *no, best not think of the possibilities.*

Creeping forward, he vaulted lightly over the low side fence and approached the broad bank of windows. All seemed still and dark – just as in the street behind him.

A small gap between the heavy drapes and the window frame allowed him to peek inside. Nothing moved. Across the room a door stood slightly ajar and through it he could see a muted light, like the glow from a television.

After scanning the street to be sure not a soul was about, he slowly reached up and tried the first window. Paint flaked under his fingertips and rained over his head.

Locked.

Stepping around a thorny bush, he reached for the second. This one seemed to give a touch. He smiled to himself even as his heart leapt. Bracing his fingers on either side of the frame, he pushed as slowly as his shaking hands would allow. A small click. His pulse accelerated as he stilled and waited for what seemed an eternity.

Nothing stirred – not even the large spider that sat crouched in its web, three inches from his face.

Using his thumbs, he gently levered the window again. This time it slid smoothly upward without a sound. With extreme patience he kept the pressure slow and even despite the flecks of powdery paint that filled his eyes. Soon he'd created enough of an opening to climb inside.

Like a gymnast on the Roman rings, he gripped the sill, hoisted himself up and edged his head through the gap. Every muscle in his upper body complained bitterly at the stress but he ignored the discomfort. The drape slid to the side as he drew his chest over the frame where he let himself come to rest.

The grittiness in his eyes made it hard to see and he had to contain his gasp once he'd adjusted to the dimly lit room. Almost directly below where he balanced, Julia lay awkwardly on a battered couch with her hands bound above her hood-covered head. In the gloom he could see the ropes that bound her were strung tightly and attached to the arms of the couch. Her ankles were also tied. The sight nauseated him, although he wasn't certain whether the sensation sprang from his anger or fear.

Jamal would pay dearly for this.

Wriggling inch by inch, he propelled his body inside until he rested half on the back of the couch, and half on the sill. He didn't dare touch her, in case she reacted in alarm and alerted the kidnappers to his presence.

"Seth?" she murmured faintly.

Too frightened to speak, he held himself completely still.

"Seth?" she repeated. "Is that you?" This time she moved her head to the side as if looking up through the hood.

"Shhh." He could hear sounds coming from the next room. "Yes it's me," he whispered, "How did you know?"

"I sensed you were close a while ago," she replied, "and I recognized your aftershave."

"I'm right above you." he said in his softest voice. "Don't move – I'm coming in and I don't want to land on top of you."

"I knew you'd come."

Edging forward, he put out his hands and slid over her, then rolled silently to the floor. Pushing himself into a kneeling position, he fumbled about until he found the end of the ropes began untying the knots. It took some time – whoever had tied them must have knotted each rope ten times; obviously wanting to ensure she couldn't escape. Once they were off, he massaged her wrists for a second before reaching for the hood. He lifted the rough hessian over her head and saw the tears glistening in her eyes.

"I knew you'd come," she repeated on a whimper as he dealt with the rope at her ankles.

Drawing her into his arms, he held her close as he tried to quiet her muted sobs. His own eyes welled but he knew they didn't have time for emotional reunions. Any second her captors could come to check on her and they'd be back to square one.

"Can you stand?" he asked in a whisper.

"I don't know – I think my kneecap is broken. I fell–" unconsciously he gripped her arms tighter, "–but I can try to walk."

Shaking his head, he cradled her in his arms and slowly stood. With small measured steps, he began the short journey to the front door.

"Going somewhere, Cuz?"

Seth's stomach clenched.

A cold hard object pressed against the soft flesh below his ear, then light flooded the room, blinding him for an instant. He eased his head around to see Jamal, hatred pouring from his black eyes, as he pointed a gun straight at him.

"Don't make it any worse – you don't want to add murder to the list, Jamal."

"Yes," Julia said gently, "if you just let us go–"

He cut her off by jabbing the muzzle of the gun into Seth's cheek. "Neither of you are going anywhere. Put her down and both of you go over to the couch and sit."

The moment Julia's feet touched the floor Jamal shoved Seth backward, then grabbed Julia's neck and held the gun to her throat.

Seth watched, powerless, as Julia's cheeks paled.

"What do you want, Jamal? Why have you done this?" Seth begged, hoping to distract his cousin from hurting Julia further.

"Let's just say it's my turn to have the power, the money and the fancy apartment." A self-satisfied smirk crossed Jamal's face. "I'll have Celine, too – after I'm done with your sweet little whore here."

Seth prepared to lunge at Jamal, but had to hold himself in check when he heard the gun's safety catch release.

Apparently pleased, Jamal waved the gun at Seth. "Over to the couch, Cuz – and no sudden moves, this gun has a hair trigger."

Seth backed up slowly. "If it's power or money you want, you can have it. I'll gladly give you everything I own, I'll sign anything you want, just let Julia go."

Jamal shook his head. "You forget, Cuz, the curse must be fulfilled. I'll have it all anyway, you gave me power of attorney; all I have to do is exercise it. You'll rot in jail for the rest of your life – what with all that money you embezzled, and of course the authorities do seem to frown on insider trading. And then there's murder." He pressed the muzzle of the gun deeper into Julia's bare throat and all remaining color drained from her face. "I'm sure I can rustle up a witness or two who saw you shoot your girlfriend when you found her in bed with another man ... or ..." his eyes lit with malice, "maybe two men."

A feral grin spread across his face and Seth wondered why he'd never before noticed the depth of his cousin's depravity.

Jamal slid the gun sensuously up over Julia's jaw and along her cheek as if it was a lover's hand until the muzzle came to rest against her temple. His other hand circled her throat more tightly.

"Ever seen what happens when you pull the trigger at such close range, Cuz?" Jamal asked in an almost hysterical voice. "It'd be a real shame to make such a mess of her pretty little face."

Julia began to struggle but Seth gave an imperceptible shake 'no'. She stilled instantly.

"Now, now, Julia," Jamal admonished, "I really don't want to have to shoot you just yet – after all, we have to put on a show for your boyfriend here. He needs to see what a real man can do with his woman."

Seth tried not to react as he watched Jamal slowly dig his fingers into either side of Julia's throat. She started to struggle again but Jamal's grip merely tightened.

From where Seth sat on the couch, he knew he'd have no chance to get to her before Jamal pulled the trigger. And he also knew Jamal's harsh fingers would soon begin to restrict the blood flow to her brain if he didn't think of something – fast.

"*Seth*?" Julia begged on a hoarse whisper.

"I'll do whatever you want," Seth pleaded, hoping to divert Jamal in any way he could. "Everything I own is yours – all of it!"

But Jamal wasn't listening and Julia began to sag in his choking hold.

The blood roared in Seth's ears. The primal desire to hurl himself across the room and rip out Jamal's heart became almost overpowering but he knew a reckless move now could see Jamal snap Julia's neck like a twig. Instead he focused on sending her a reassuring smile. His chest ached with impotent rage as his gaze locked onto Jamal's black eyes – inwardly he vowed his cousin would pay. Painfully.

Julia was flagging. Seth prayed that help to arrive soon.

Where the hell was Rick? And Kirkman?

Surely one of them had entered the house by now.

Julia whimpered. Eyes wide and glassy, all the fight seemed to have gone out of her. She barely breathed and her face grew more gray and ghost-like with each passing second. She began to slump in his cousin's arms and Seth felt a wave of relief when Jamal was forced to release her throat to keep her upright.

Yet he managed to hold the gun to her head the entire time.

Seth wanted to scream with frustration.

Tilting his head to the side without once taking his eyes from Seth, Jamal yelled toward the next room. "Hey, Gerry! Get out here – time for a bit of fun!"

He grinned over at Seth as if he was sharing a well-kept secret. "He's been itching to get into her pants for ages, you know. Wanted to have some fun earlier, but I wouldn't let him – better to take your time and savor the moment. Besides, I wanted to have first go at her."

Swallowing back the rage he felt, Seth's fists clenched rhythmically, tingling in anticipation of the moment when they'd close around Jamal's neck and squeeze until he ceased to breathe.

With his attention focused wholly on Seth, Jamal didn't notice that when Gerry finally entered the room behind him, he was gagged and handcuffed to Kirkman.

Seth kept his eyes as steady as he could – a gun was still pressed to Julia's temple.

"Tie Seth up, Gerry. He can watch while we both enjoy his woman." Jamal said with a smug expression, still blissfully unaware that his comrade wasn't in a position to follow orders. "We'll deliver him to the cops as soon as we hear they've issued the warrant for his arrest – shouldn't be more than another day or two. That gives us plenty of time to have some fun. Heck, Celine can even join in if she wants. Celine! Come join us, sweetie, we're about to play a few games while we wait for the cops to arrest your former lover."

Seth's lips twitched as he attempted to suppress his growing sense of relief. "Don't think your plan'll work," he said, deliberately baiting Jamal.

"Why not?" he curled his lip derisively, "– all the evidence will say you're guilty. I reckon you'll be locked up for a decade or more, even if we don't kill your whore – and in the meantime..."

None too gently, Rick shoved Celine into the room alongside the hapless Gerry. Her mouth was covered with black gaffer tape and her wrists were bound. Panic filled her eyes.

An ominous click sounded at the back of Jamal's head. "Like the man said," Kirkman whispered in a lethal tone, "I don't think your plan'll work."

As Jamal spun about to see who had spoken, Seth launched himself at his cousin, kicking the gun from his hand and wresting Julia from his grasp in a single motion. They rolled to the floor as the gun went off, the bullet harmlessly hitting the wall alongside Gerry's foot.

Gerry's eyes widened before he crumpled to the floor in a dead faint.

The front door crashed open.

Tobias stood braced in the portal, brandishing a sawn-off shotgun aimed straight at Kirkman. "Hold it right there!"

He strode into the room to stand over Seth and Julia as they lay on the floor. The sound as he cocked the rifle seemed to echo.

The room went completely silent and for a long moment nobody moved.

Kirkman kept his gun trained on Jamal. "I'd say it's a stalemate," he said to Tobias. "Who d'you reckon'll be faster – me or you?"

Jamal slumped as if defeated.

"I don't give a shit – kill him for all I care. I just came along for the ride. And for Julia." Tobias said as he swung the shotgun down until it pointed straight at Seth's back. "At this range I won't even need to aim."

Kirkman held his ground and didn't so much as blink. "If you shoot him, you'll kill her as well."

"No I won't. Julia–" Tobias held out a hand to her as if she were a child, "–come to me. Slowly. We'll just take our leave – that way nobody'll get hurt."

Seth could feel Julia trembling as she began to edge from under him. "I can't let him hurt you," she whispered, tears streaming unchecked.

But Seth held her tight and brushed his lips against her cheek. "It's okay babe – I won't let him take you," he said, knowing his words might well tip Tobias over the edge.

Seth wouldn't release his hold on her. "Not again," he whispered. "This time I won't let them win." The reassurance in his eyes was enough. Julia fixed her gaze on his, trusting him to save her.

Hoping Seth's words had drawn Tobias's attention, Kirkman turned lightning fast and pointed the pistol at Tobias's forehead.

Tobias sneered as if unconcerned and shoved the shotgun against Seth's back in warning. His finger caressed the trigger. "Don't push me or I will kill him – her too if necessary."

Kirkman looked over at Rick and nodded then began inching backward, careful to keep Jamal in his sights.

Celine began to squeal incoherently beneath the gaffer tape.

"Shut up, you stupid bitch!" Tobias growled at her. Celine shook her head frantically and squealed again, but Tobias was more intent on Julia. "Come here Julia. If you want him to live, you'll come to me. Now!"

Three uniformed policemen had crept into the room behind Tobias, each with pistols aimed at his head.

"Behind you," Kirkman said, grinning widely.

Tobias looked one way then the other. Then, after a long moment of indecision, allowed the shotgun to slide the floor.

As the police cuffed his hands behind him, he stared at Julia. "You shouldn't have run from me – I would never have hurt you."

Julia turned away and buried her head in Seth's shoulder.

Epilogue

The Nile

Three weeks later...

"Bye! Have fun!" Julia called as the boat pulled away from the Luxor dock. Tears traveled down her cheeks.

Seth grinned. "Why, the heck, are you crying? You'll see them in less than a month for the wedding."

"Yeah, I know. It's just ... "

Seth swung her into his arms. "C'mon, let's get back to the hotel. If you behave, I promise to make love to you before dinner."

She gave him a playful punch on the shoulder even as her lips lifted in that secret smile she always wore when she had seduction in mind. As they walked the paths that Seth's ancestors undoubtedly walked, Julia wondered whether she'd have met Seth at all, if it weren't for the tragic events in the life of the young princess all those thousands of years ago....

*

If you liked *The Curse*, read Julia and Seth's prequel, *Warrior King*, the tragic story of their ancestors, Alia and Pharaoh Tuthmosis.

Other Titles by Jennifer Brassel
Trust in Dreams
Secret Reflection
Warrior King
Honour Bound
Writing as J A Lesley:
Coins of Power
Available from all good online booksellers

Also by Jennifer Brassel

Honour Bound
Trust in Dreams
Secret Reflection
The Curse

Watch for more at www.jenniferbrassel.com.

About the Author

Jenny Brassel is passionate about a lot of things: history, mythology and romance to name but a few, and writing allows her imagination to run riot. Creative to the bone, when Jennifer isn't writing she can be seen with a paintbrush in hand.

History, especially ancient history, is her most fervent passion and recently she has spread her writing wings to pen the first in a series of historical sagas based around the lives of her favourite pharaohs. They are filled with the epic stories of life in ancient times, warts, brutality and all.

Her work has won a number of major romance writing contests including the Land of Enchantment Romance Writers' *Rebecca;* From The Heart Romance Writers' *Wallflower* and Missouri Romance Writers of America's *Gateway to the Best.*

Jenny holds an MA in Creative Writing and teaches courses and workshops for community colleges and writing centres.

Jenny hails from Sydney Australia. Married to her high school sweetheart, most of her days are spent staring at her computer screen under the supervision of a very demanding bichon frisé, Cordy.

Read more at www.jenniferbrassel.com.